Renee,

MISS BELIEF

AUBREY BONDURANT

It's no longer pretend!

♡ Aubrey Bondurant

This is a work of fiction. Names, characters, businesses, places, events, and incidents are either the products of the author's imagination or used in a fictitious manner. Any resemblance to actual persons, living or dead, or actual events is purely coincidental.

This book is for mature audiences only.
Cover by Marisa @ Cover Me Darlings
Text copyright © 2020 by Aubrey Bondurant
ISBN-13 : 979-8695484588

Sign up for my newsletter for all the latest release information HERE

Chapter One

TEAGAN

My hangover mocked me for deciding to drink so much last night. And why the hell did my big toe ache too? Blurry visions of tripping over the coffee table while attempting a goofy dance move in my living room drifted back to me. Thank you, drunken archives, for the memory.

My roommate wasn't faring much better from our two pitchers of regret.

Chloe gave me a wan smile as I helped her haul her suitcases outside our apartment building to the taxi waiting to take her to the Dubai airport. It was an ungodly hour, before sunrise. I would've driven her, but we'd traded our ability to operate a motor vehicle for vodka.

"I'll miss you," she murmured.

"I'll miss you too. Let me know once you get settled in LA." I wasn't normally a hugger, but for my best friend, I'd make an exception.

She pulled back with a smirk. "Will do. Please tell me you'll do what we talked about last night and finally make a move on Reid."

Did we talk about my crush last night? Details were hazy.

"Not happening, Chloe Bear." Even if I wasn't a big old chicken about making the first move, I could think of at least a hundred reasons it was a bad idea. "In case you forgot, he's now my boss."

She sighed. "So what? He's single, and it may be your last shot given that you'll probably be leaving Dubai in a few months. You promised last night you were going to do something."

"It was the vodka talking." Despite the object of my secret obsession recently becoming single, he definitely wasn't over his ex by evidence of the way he'd been insufferably moody ever since his breakup. Plus, the whole point of a crush was being infatuated with someone who wasn't attainable. Breakup or not, Reid Maxwell was way out of my league. Nope. I was definitely not up for rejection. He would have to stay a harmless infatuation. "Safe travels, Chloe Bear."

"Nice subject change. I'll text you once I arrive."

I gave Chloe one last hug before watching her climb into the back seat of the car, tears visible on her face. I may have stood there dry eyed, but on the inside I was a wreck. I'd never had a best friend before my soon-to-be-former roommate, and having her move seven thousand miles away to the other side of the world was doing weird things to me. Making me emotional and shit.

I was also happy for her. Chloe was pursuing her dream to go back to college despite her recent heartbreak. Her boyfriend, Aiden, evidently needed to chase his demons before he could commit to her.

As for me, I'd continue to stay in Dubai for at least a few more months to help my sister pay off the debt racked up by my niece's cancer treatment. That was why I'd taken the contract job here with Delmont Security in the first place.

At least Penelope was now cancer-free. If you ever needed proof how life could suck, take the example of a four-year-old having to fight leukemia. It didn't matter if I had to work two jobs on the other side of the world to help pay for her treatments. I'd do it ten times over if it meant my beautiful niece could live the life she deserved.

As I slowly traipsed back into the building and up the elevator to my floor, I was tempted to call in sick today. But if I did, it would mean sitting in my horribly empty apartment and feeling sorry for myself. Nope, I'd pull on my big-girl britches, tame my unruly red hair into a bun, wear black to reflect my mood, and tackle the day.

The day which included seeing my crush. My all-consuming, borderline-obsessive, definitely unhealthy crush.

My infatuation was inconvenient at best, and depressing at worst.

I recalled the first time I'd met Reid Maxwell. Of course I'd instantly thought he was handsome. Who wouldn't think so with his dark hair, boyish face, and easy smile? He had dimples that did something to my stomach whenever he flashed them. But it was the way he'd been so damn polite and kind in our initial meeting which stuck out the most. I'd never been around a man my age who hadn't objectified me in some way. Some men were subtle, others not so much, but Reid had never once stared at my chest, nor had he spoken down to me. He'd been part of the recruiting team at the time, and I remember his interview being my favorite as he'd put me right at ease. Unlike some of the other directors working for Delmont, Reid never put on airs or treated people like his title made him better than anyone else.

He was both a gentleman and sexy as hell, a combination

responsible for instigating my infatuation. I'd known he had a girlfriend and then he'd gotten engaged, making him off-limits. But now, a year later, here I was working for him. And as of six weeks ago, he was quite single.

In theory, I should've loved the opportunity to have daily interaction with the man who'd fueled many a nighttime fantasy and, frankly, a few daytime ones too. But since his breakup, he'd been a mopey, miserable mess, which made daily interaction with him nothing short of torture.

Where was the old Reid?

I drove into the office in my leased red Jeep Wrangler, already missing my roommate and our morning talks on the fifteen-minute drive into the office. Surveying the traffic, I took note of all the other SUVs on the road. In the city of Dubai, no one cared about gas prices as they were ridiculously low. My only requirement for a vehicle was air-conditioning. Of all things you couldn't live without in the desert, AC was at the top of the list, even in early spring. Come summer, there'd be no living without it because of the horrible humidity, despite being the desert.

I didn't bother to put my face on until after I arrived at the office, spending a few minutes in the ladies' room to carefully apply my makeup. I could say the effort was because I wanted to hide the effects of my wicked hangover, but it was more about my boss and the sad fact I always wanted to look my best for him.

Pathetic, wasn't it? Yet the minute he approached our little corner of the twentieth floor, walking past the rows of cubes, my breath caught in my throat. I was reminded yet again of how annoying it was to have a crush on my boss.

He gave me a slight nod as he started to walk by my desk, a bag in hand and a frown on his face.

Ugh, we'd gone from chatty Reid, who was always quick

with a smile, to mopey Reid, who barely made eye contact, to now a "fuck you" head-nod Reid. As on most recent mornings, he appeared decidedly hungover with red eyes and a puffy face.

"Good morning, Reid. How was your night?" I tried each day to drag him into conversation. One he used to be interested in having.

"Fine. Thanks." He stepped into his office and shut the door, letting it be known he didn't give a shit to reciprocate any interest in my life.

"My evening was good too, but Chloe left this morning, and so I'm sad, which is an emotion I have a hard time with, but thanks for asking. Really appreciate it."

Asshole. There was no heat to my internal thought as it wasn't actually true. Or at least he'd never shown these asshole tendencies before the breakup. I shook my head, missing the considerate, funny, friendly Reid.

I contemplated many ways I could broach the subject of his attitude. But thoughtfulness in speaking was not a skill I possessed. In other words, I didn't know how to tell him, with tact and grace, to get his shit together.

Hoping to get my mind off it all, I began perusing my email until someone approached.

"Teagan, right?"

The voice belonged to a handsome young guy with an easy smile. I thought I recognized him perhaps working in Technical Support? Was his name Ned or Ted? I couldn't remember if we'd ever been officially introduced.

His eyes, which had zoned in on my breasts, finally wandered up to my face. *There you go, buddy, my eyes are up here.* In his defense, my perfect C cups were hard to ignore on my tall, thin frame. Guess I had one thing for which to thank my worthless mother.

Although boob-gazer blondie was cute with his big brown eyes, he wasn't winning any points with his lack of eye contact. But at least he was blushing as though he hadn't meant to ogle.

"Yes. I'm Teagan."

"I'm Fred. I work in Tech Support, and have seen you around."

I tended to stick out, being the only five-foot-ten, red-haired, pale-skinned girl in the entire building. And considering I lived in the company's corporate housing, it made sense we'd probably seen each other at some point. "Yes, you look familiar, Fred. What can I help you with?"

"Um, I'm not quite sure how to say this."

Was he about to ask me out? I was about to tell him I didn't date people I work with when he surprised me.

"It's about your boss."

My brows shot up. "What about him?"

"Well, last night I was working the midnight-to-nine a.m. shift when Mr. Maxwell called because he couldn't remember his password. No big deal except he couldn't seem to follow instructions over the phone for resetting it, so I came up here to his office in order to help. I noticed the strong smell of alcohol on his breath. He seemed like he'd had a few too many."

My lips flattened. I'd suspected Reid of drinking at night by his hungover appearance each morning, but this was beyond what was acceptable. Sure, I was hungover this morning too, but the alcohol was out of my system by the time I entered the building. "What time was this?"

"About two o'clock in the morning."

Reid had no reason to be in the office at that hour. No international calls. No extra work I knew of. "Did you tell anyone else?"

Fred's head was already shaking. "No. Mr. Maxwell has always been nice to me. Remembers my name when other directors don't bother to recall anyone below the title of manager. Anyhow, I don't know what's going on with him, but I wanted to share it with you in case there's something you could maybe do. I'd hate to see anything happen if it were to be another analyst who helps him next time."

I was instantly grateful. "Thank you for your discretion. Yes. He's, uh, going through some personal stuff."

He sighed. "I figured. And hey, at least he didn't drive drunk."

Considering the strict laws in Dubai, I imagined the penalty for driving drunk would be severe. "Thanks for helping him. And for coming to me."

"Sure. Take care."

I sat there for a full minute after Fred left processing what he'd said. I couldn't not say something to Reid now. This was it. It was the limit.

It was time for an intervention.

Chapter Two

REID

I walked into my office, ignoring the impressive view of the Dubai cityscape even though it was painted pink and yellow from the sunrise. Shutting the door, I flopped into my desk chair, and briefly cradled my head in my hands. In dire need of relief, I reached over to open the package I'd just bought downstairs and tore through the box in search of two magic pills of Advil. A hangover to start the day was fast becoming a habit I wasn't proud of, and this morning's was worse than usual.

But the nights had proved long, and sleep had proved difficult. That's why last night, instead of going home to a depressingly empty apartment, I'd chosen to return to the office after having a few too many bourbons at the steakhouse next door. I hadn't accomplished a whole lot in the way of work, except locking myself out of my computer after several bad attempts at my password, but at least I hadn't stared at the ceiling in my bedroom all night.

I couldn't remember the last time I'd had a full night's sleep, gone to the gym, or eaten anything remotely healthy. I hadn't spoken with any of my friends in forever because I didn't want to talk about the breakup. Didn't wish to rehash the scandal.

No, thank you. I didn't need to hear the pity in their voices or be reminded of the humiliation.

During the last couple of months, it felt as if I was in the movie *Groundhog Day*, waking to the same day, over and over again. Although it wasn't the first time Vanessa and I had broken up over the years, it was definitely the only time I knew without a doubt there would be no reconciliation. I couldn't. Not after discovering my fiancée in an upstairs bathroom at a family holiday party, down on her knees in front of my older brother and his unzipped pants. It was a scene forever etched in my mind. Like a car crash, everything had happened so quickly I could barely register the impact.

I'd immediately grabbed my things, bolted from the house, and boarded a plane from Boston to Dubai the same night. Mini bottle after mini bottle had drowned my sorrows during the flight. Of course Vanessa had called incessantly the first few days after it had happened, begging and pleading for forgiveness, but it wasn't something I could offer. Even weeks later, I was still angry. Angry with her. And angry with my brother. Two of the most significant relationships I'd ever had wrecked in one moment.

At first, I'd been shocked and devastated, but lately I'd transitioned into a much more comfortable state of numbness. This phase had me changing my phone number to dodge my ex's incessant calls, avoiding my family, friends, and coworkers, and drinking until I no longer felt any hurt or betrayal.

Although we were polar opposites, my older brother, Chance, had always been someone I'd looked up to and respected. Someone I'd counted on to be there for me when times got tough or our family got crazy. He'd always supported my need to do things for myself and not rely on our family's money. Hell, he'd been the poster child for living independently. And as such, I'd idolized him as a kid.

But what did you do when the one person you always turned to was the same person who'd let you down?

You took two Advil and pretended not to care.

Now if only they had a pill to ease my ever-growing guilt when it came to Teagan. Each morning she would smile and ask me how my night was, and each day I'd barely speak a couple of words to her. My behavior was on the dickish spectrum for sure, and I was surprised she'd put up with it for as long as she had, given how she wasn't normally one to mind her tongue.

At least my work hadn't suffered. I'd thrown myself into it, trying to drown my heartbreak by keeping busy.

My phone buzzed with the head of my division, a man by the name of Gary Denton. "Hi, Mr. Denton, how are you?" I greeted, wincing at the sound of my own voice piercing my massive headache.

"Good, Reid, good. Wanted to call up and see if you've given any more consideration to the promotion opportunity in the Sydney office?"

Before my breakup with Vanessa, I wouldn't have contemplated the move at all, since we'd planned to move to New York City, but now— Well, now a fresh start in a new country sounded like just the thing I needed. "Yes, I have. I'm going to put in for it."

"Good. Glad to hear it. They could use someone with your experience down under. Send me an email once you've filled out your application. But do it soon because the job opening closes at the end of the week."

"Will do. What do you think my chances are?"

"Good, especially when I put in a word for you."

"It's appreciated." While some directors were here to

make money and didn't bother to cultivate relationships, I'd always felt strongly about genuinely getting to know people and forge connections with them.

"Take care."

"Thanks. You too."

I sat there for a full minute contemplating my poor life choices of late until a knock on my door had me straighten and flinch at the sound. I couldn't keep drinking this way.

"Come in."

Teagan peeked her face in. "I need to speak with you."

My glance at the clock confirmed I didn't have time. I was booked all morning. "I have a call in two minutes. Can it wait until lunch?"

Her lips pursed. "Fine. We'll talk then."

Dread tingled down my spine at her serious tone. "Can I ask what it concerns?"

"It concerns the removal of your head from your ass."

Chapter Three
TEAGAN

*T*ypically, Reid's post-breakup lunch consisted of a double cheeseburger, side of fries, and a large Coca-Cola. Every single day.

Which is why today I instead got him a chicken Caesar salad and a bottle of water.

That was the meal the old Reid had eaten for lunch—I knew because I'd researched every detail of his life during my borderline stalking of him over the last year. And since I was about to officially stage an intervention, I was going full in. Starting with the damn salad.

I was still angry about the information Fred had given me this morning. What in the hell had Reid been thinking to be drunk at work? Worse, to be drunk at work as a director of security in a country with strict penalties against public drunkenness. It was beyond stupid. He could lose his clearance and his job. I might be tolerant of heartbroken, mopey, and even dickish Reid. But stupid Reid? Nope.

I'd reached my limit. I wouldn't sit back and watch him piss away his career on a cheating ex-fiancée who had never deserved him to begin with.

MISS BELIEF

As I raised my free hand to knock on his door, a lump the size of a golf ball formed in my throat. Although I often spoke my mind, I certainly didn't go out of my way to make someone feel bad. But my intentions didn't always line up with my behavior. Sigh. Let's hope this time could be different.

When he answered my knock with a "come in," I entered with lunch in hand. Reid glanced up from his computer, pausing a moment in his phone conversation to focus his deep blue eyes on me.

My stomach clenched with his attention.

Here at Delmont Security, he was responsible for commercial security. This consisted of designing security systems for high-end hotels and businesses. Since he'd been out of the billable role for the last year while filling in for the HR director, he was starting fresh with a number of new business pitches. From the sound of his conversation, he was finishing up a successful sales call now.

My eyes were drawn to the cityscape of Dubai, visible from his office window. I remember being in awe when I'd first arrived. The grandeur in the desert was a sight to see with all of the incredibly tall buildings and wealth on display.

Shifting my gaze, I focused on the corner of Reid's desk where a giant, framed picture of his fiancée used to sit.

I wondered what he'd done with the photo. Was it in his desk drawer for him to pine over every time he opened it? Broken into little pieces from throwing it against the wall, or had he simply tossed it in the bin for someone to wonder what had inspired such an action? There was no guessing between the many possible outcomes if it had been me. Option two for the win.

He hung up the phone before glancing at the contents of his lunch tray. Sitting back in his chair, he appeared mildly amused. "I suppose getting me a salad instead of a burger is tied to your earlier statement today about removing my head from my ass."

"Yup. It's step one for ass removal."

There was a hint of a smile around his lips when I took a seat across from his desk in the visitor's chair.

"And what, pray tell, has brought this newfound interest in where my head is located?"

Blunt but tactful, Teagan. You can do this.

"I know you're going through a breakup, and I care about you—" More than he would ever know.

He leaned forward, forearms on his desk, scowl firmly in place. "Cut the feeling-sorry-for-me crap and spit it out, Teagan."

My temper spiked. "Fine, first your reaction right there is that of a jerk. I don't feel sorry for you. I know you're dealing with a breakup and coping the best way you can, but you can't keep acting the way you have. I'm trying to be fucking delicate here."

A chuckle broke from his lips. "Fucking delicate like a Mack truck."

I cracked a smile. "Yeah, well…"

He let out a long sigh before running a hand over his face. "I realize I've been off lately."

"You were drunk last night. In the office."

His eyes went wide while his face took on an unmistakable blush. "Why would you say that?"

"Fred in Tech Support said you forgot your password, and when you couldn't follow instructions over the phone, he came up here to your office. He could smell the alcohol on you, Reid. And he came by this morning to talk to me because he doesn't want it to be someone else next time, someone who might go to HR instead."

"Terrific," he muttered.

I leaned forward, placing my elbows on his desk. "You're going through a rough time. I get it. And I thought seeing you mopey was bad, but seeing you cold and indifferent is worse."

"I realize I haven't been easy to work for these last few weeks."

"Dirty-sock-and-Mento-smelling Andy in Accounting was more fun."

"Jesus. I was striving for comfortably numb."

"You overshot into near asshole territory. And self-medicating with alcohol could cost you your career."

I didn't miss the way his face blanched.

"You're right. It could. I need to find Fred and apologize."

"You can if you want. Either way, I don't believe he'll say anything. But the heavy drinking needs to stop. I know you're my boss, but you're also my friend." Or at least friendly. "I had my first hangover in forever this morning, so I can't imagine how miserable it would be to come into the office with one on a daily basis."

He cocked his head to the side, flashing me his killer boyish grin, reminiscent of the Reid of the past. "Why were you drunk on a random Sunday night?"

"I blame Sex in the Driveway."

What was great about Reid was the way he always took my crazy in stride. As if it amused him to hear what might come out of my mouth. It had been awhile since he'd engaged in conversation with me.

"Mm, I may need more details, if I'm allowed to ask."

"The drink's name is Sex in the Driveway, it's like Sex on the Beach, but with vodka, peach schnapps, and blue curacao instead of the cranberry juice. I call it sweet, but deadly.

Anyhow two pitchers of cocktails during Chloe's last night here, and I had a wicked hangover."

"Chloe went back to LA?"

I nodded.

"I'm sorry to hear it. I know you guys were close."

This. This was the guy I missed. "There he is."

He didn't bother to pretend he wasn't aware of what I was talking about. "I'm sorry. I understand how it feels to lose your best friend. Hell, Aiden would be kicking my ass if he were here."

"Apology accepted. And I'm sorry for what you've been going through."

"You have nothing to be sorry for."

"Anything I can help with?"

He picked up a card from his desk. "Any chance you can fast-forward through this wedding I have to go to in two weeks where I'll see the ex?"

"I'm fresh out of that particular superpower. But, wait, I thought the wedding wasn't until this summer. Or is it a different one?"

What could I say? I was nosey and had learned of the impending "see-the-ex wedding" through Chloe.

"It's a different wedding between my college friend and Vanessa's cousin that was originally scheduled for next year. They had to move it up because of a surprise pregnancy. Now it's a beach wedding at a resort in Turks and Caicos under the guise of suddenly desiring a destination venue instead. But lucky me, I'll have another wedding to go to in June where I'll see the ex too." He paused before expelling a frustrated breath. "So give it to me straight—how will it go?"

"Well, if your intention is to go to the wedding and look as though you've been absolutely miserable and clearly aren't over your ex, then mission accomplished."

His jaw locked. "And if that's not what I want?"

"You need to stop drinking. Stop moping. Get your mind off of her and at least appear to have moved on. We can come up with a plan."

His brow quirked. "We?"

"I thought I'd offer my assistance, but if I'm being too oversteppy, then I'll back off."

"It might be nice to have someone who keeps me from being a mopey almost asshole. Aside from ditching the cheeseburgers, what else needs to be part of my plan to at least appear I'm over my ex?"

"Get some sleep, go to the gym, and get a haircut."

He ran his hands over his silky locks making me wish my hands were touching him instead. Maybe I should re-evaluate my suggestion for him to get a haircut. He was adorable as it was.

"So what you're telling me is I've turned into an overweight, shaggy, sleepy alcoholic."

"Self-deprecation will not solve the issue. You simply need to start taking better care of yourself. You're—" Incredibly hot, too adorable for words, battery-operated-friend worthy. "You're still a nice-looking guy."

He let out a deep chuckle. "Don't worry. Just because I'm holding on to your compliment like the last crumb of my self-esteem doesn't mean I'm weird about it."

We both grinned at his humor.

"Glad to hear it."

His grin faded, and he heaved a heavy sigh. "This wedding is a disaster waiting to happen. Everyone there will be hoping we'll reconcile."

As much as it pained me to ask, I had to know. "Do you want to get back together?"

"No."

He didn't elaborate, but his resolute answer was a relief. Nevertheless, I absolutely hated the idea of him attending a wedding alone with everyone plotting to get him and his ex back together.

"Maybe you should take another woman with you as your date for the weekend." I tamped down on my jealousy as I made the suggestion.

"Yeah, like who?"

I shrugged. "I don't know. Maybe someone you previously dated? It would certainly send a message if you brought an ex-girlfriend to a destination wedding."

"I've never had another girlfriend."

My eyes went wide. "Never?" Reid was thirty-two years old, about to turn thirty-three on September tenth—because yeah, I'd been obsessed with him long enough to have learned that sort of detail. But I certainly hadn't thought his fiancée was the only woman he'd ever dated.

His face flushed. "I dated other people, you know, in between the breakups, but it wasn't ever serious with anyone else. Definitely not anyone I could call up out of the blue and invite to a destination wedding two weeks away."

In between the breakups. The words bounced in my brain. How many times had he and his fiancée broken up and gotten back together? Sounded as if it was their pattern. No wonder people might believe they'd reconcile yet again.

"Any chance you can skip the wedding altogether?"

"I'm a groomsman, and frankly speaking, pride won't let me bow out, so no. But your suggestion of taking a date could work if…" His face lit up with whatever idea he had.

"If what?"

His expression lit up. "If you'll go with me."

Chapter Four

REID

This was either the best or worst idea I'd ever had. But the more I rolled it around in my head, the more I was convinced taking Teagan with me to the wedding would be perfect.

One, I wouldn't have to worry about her getting attached. She clearly found me pathetic, given she'd felt she had to stage an intervention. Two, she would be a great ally to have with me when I saw my ex for the first time since the cheating scandal. And three, she could kick my ass if I acted like a mopey idiot again.

"Me?" she asked, uncharacteristically blushing.

I'd known Teagan over a year, and frankly, I didn't think anything fazed her. She'd make the perfect fake girlfriend for a crowd that included my college friends, my family, and my ex.

"Yes, you could pretend to be my new girlfriend. After all, it was your suggestion."

"But I live here in Dubai."

"Which is what makes it believable. People would buy the fact we work together and recently started dating." I pushed to my feet, suddenly full of energy. For the first time in weeks, I felt something other than dread over this wedding. "I'll fly you there. It's a weekend event, so maybe we'd arrive on Thursday, then leave on Monday. Or your sister lives in California, right? I could fly you to see her afterwards for a few days if you want."

"Yes, my sister lives in LA. But I'm not sure anyone would believe I'm your girlfriend."

"Why the hell not?" Teagan was one of the most beautiful women I'd ever met. Ivory skin with a smidge of freckles she tried to cover with makeup, dark red, curly hair she often wore up, and a body that could make a grown man weep. Best of all, she was confident and wouldn't crumble under the scrutiny of my crazy family, not to mention Vanessa and her catty friends. And she hadn't been afraid to call me out when I'd been spiraling.

I'd spent most of my life loving the same woman, and now post-breakup, I simply didn't know what to do with myself. But taking a date like Teagan to the wedding would send a clear message that reconciliation was off the table. It would show I was moving on.

She shook her head. "I don't know if I could pull it off. I mean we don't—we're not—we'd have to fake stuff—"

There it was again. The flush in her cheeks. My face heated to match when I thought of all the things we'd be faking. What had I been thinking? I was placing her in an incredibly awkward position especially since I was her boss.

"On second thought, forget it. I was getting ahead of myself and am putting you on the spot. I'm sorry. I appreciate you being honest with me. I'm planning to give up the daily drinking, the fast food, and maybe I'll even hit the gym. And from here on out, I'll try to pull my head out and be less miserable. I'd hate to see you choose Mentos-and-dirty-sock-smelling Andy in Accounting over me."

She giggled, the sound reminding me how much I'd missed her sense of humor.

"I'd be happy to become your gym buddy. With Chloe gone, I don't have one, either."

"I'll consider it." My motivation for hitting the gym before the wedding had suddenly evaporated. "Thank you. You know, for being honest with me."

She stood up, a myriad of emotions playing out on her face. "You're welcome. Okay, then. I'll talk to you later."

Once she left, I thumped my head on my desk. I'd never dreaded seeing my friends and family like I did right now. The whole thing made me crave a drink, but I couldn't keep leaning on the alcohol to numb myself. Teagan had been spot-on about my stunt last night. It had been beyond stupid. I'd put my job at risk. It would've been too easy to send the wrong email or say the wrong thing. I was humiliated that my actions had caused another professional to come to my assistant with his concerns.

It was tempting to bow out of the wedding. I'm sure no one would blame me considering the date had been moved up and the venue changed, but pride wouldn't allow me to go that route. No, I would go there with my head held high.

Things needed to change. Starting today.

Chapter Five

TEAGAN

After leaving Reid's office, I sat at my desk stunned. He'd asked me to be his fake girlfriend, and I'd turned him down. God, just imagining the excuse to hold his hand and kiss him was giving me heart palpitations. How could I become a fake girlfriend with a man I'd dreamed about for a whole year? There's no way I could pull it off. And even if I could, it would most likely turn into a heartbreak train wreck.

Or would it?

Could I fake it while keeping my true feelings to myself? Here I'd been waiting for an opportunity where he could see me as more than a coworker. What if this was it? What if this was the chance to take our relationship from friendly coworkers to more? But wasn't it too soon after his breakup?

Yes. Undoubtedly he wasn't ready for another relationship given how down he was about the end of his last one.

By the time I'd left the office for the night, I was still obsessing over it. Evaluating the pros and cons of becoming his fake girlfriend when I had real feelings.

An hour later, I had changed into my comfy clothes and

was sitting in the lonely living room of my two-bedroom apartment with the walls painted an awful shade of corporate-housing beige. But my smile came easily when a familiar FaceTime number flashed up on my cell phone.

My sister's beautiful face came into focus when I hit the accept button. Whereas the sun was enemy number one on my fair skin, it turned Tory into a beach goddess with her golden glow.

"Hi, Tory," I greeted.

"Hi. Sorry, I meant to call you this weekend, but time got away from me. You free to say hello to Penelope?"

With the eleven-hour time difference between here and Los Angeles, and both of us working weekend nights, it was difficult to connect with home. But I always had time to say hello to my adorable niece. "Of course. I'm just home from work. Put her on."

"Hi, Aunty T."

My grin went big at Penelope's adorable face. Blue eyes, rosy cheeks, and a smile for days. I might be biased, but I thought my niece was the prettiest little girl on the planet. "Hi, Penny. How are you?"

"Good, but my hair isn't growing back yet."

My breath stuck in my throat. What did you say to a four-year-old who'd gone through a round of treatment for leukemia, and who'd lost all her hair as a result? "It'll take some time, but once it does grow back, it'll be beautiful."

"Mama says the same thing. When it gets longer, will you braid it? Like a princess?"

"Anything for you." Tears formed at the thought. I didn't grow up with religion, but since her diagnosis, I'd prayed for her recovery, and sincerely hoped this was the end of her treatments. As of last week, she was officially in remission, but the next few months were critical in testing to confirm the chemo had worked, and the cancer didn't return. I could only hope a God who'd never paid much attention to my family would finally take notice and grant this one prayer to keep her in remission.

"It'll be long and blond like your mama's hair."

"I hope it grows back red like yours."

Funny how some kids could be so sweet while others could be so mean. My fiery red hair had meant torture through most of my adolescence. I could only assume that since both my mother and Tory had blond hair, my hair color had come from my father. Now that we were adults and thanks to a DNA test, my sister and I knew we didn't share that side of the gene pool.

"Any color of hair would be pretty on you."

"What funny shirt are you wearing today?" she asked in her sweet little, childlike voice.

Among my few prized possessions was a collection of funny, sarcastic, and sometimes inappropriate T-shirts. Thankfully, the one I currently wore was suitable for my niece. It was one of my favorites. I moved it into the picture. "It says, 'Cute But Psycho.'"

She shrugged, either not getting it or not thinking it was funny. Tough crowd. "Okay. I'm gonna go watch *Frozen 2*. Here's Mama. Love you. Bye."

I adored the way she switched tasks on a whim, but was left viewing the ceiling as she must've set the phone down on something. "Love you too. Hello?"

Tory's face came into view as she picked up the phone. Sometimes it was hard to remember she was the older sister considering how youthful she looked, despite her tired eyes. "I'm here. Work going okay? Your mopey boss still mopey? Or wait— You said he morphed into dick territory last time we talked, yeah?"

Victoria knew all about my crush on Reid, but I wasn't about to share the details of today's intervention, not when I needed her advice on something entirely different. "It may be turning around. He has a wedding in a couple weeks where he'll see the ex, and when I told him he should consider taking a date, he asked if maybe I'd go."

Her brows went sky high. "What did you say?"

I exhaled my frustration, still upset about how I'd reacted. "I was in shock, so I sort of made excuses, and he apologized and told me to never mind."

"What do you want to do? Be honest."

As if I'd ever lie to my sister. She was a single mom who'd been through a parent's worst nightmare with her child battling cancer. There was no hiding my bullshit from her. I hadn't been able to do so when I was a kid, a teenager, or even now; nor was there any doubt she would always be on my side.

"Of course I want to do it. But I don't think he's over his ex-fiancée by a long shot. He revealed they've broken up multiple times, and all his friends and family will be expecting them to get back together."

"But I thought his ex sucked his older brother's dick."

Like me, Tory didn't have much of a filter. A hard life did that to you. It took away your ability to sugarcoat things. "Yes, and he says he doesn't want her back."

"You still in love with him?"

My face burned at her question. "I'm not in love with him. It's a silly crush."

One where I knew way too much information about him to be considered healthy, but I wasn't in love with him. Pfft.

Jesus, did I really just do a mental pfft?

Her smirk was annoyingly perceptive. "In that case, then, you should pretend to be his girlfriend and get over it."

"What do you mean get over it?"

"Crushes are based on infatuation. Infatuation is based on not really knowing someone. When he was engaged, he was off-limits, making it easy to keep things surface level and believe it couldn't happen. So I'd argue if you get to know him better now, and there's no longer the unattainable factor, you may be able to get over this crush. Demystify him and truly get to know him. Knock him off the pedestal you put him on and bring him down to the level of the rest of us mortals. That is, if you want to."

I'd had a crush on Reid for so long it was hard to remember not being obsessed with him. But what if getting to know him better made him more appealing? What if my crush ended up turning into more?

"I don't want to get hurt," I admitted.

She sighed. "If you're afraid you may get hurt, then it means your feelings are deeper than a crush, and you have to ask whether it's worth the risk. As you said, it doesn't sound like he's over his ex, not by a long shot."

Even if he was over his relationship, I was nowhere near Reid's type, judging by his ex. If his taste in women was a cheese, his ex was brie while I was Cheez Whiz.

"Where is the wedding?"

"Turks and Caicos. He offered to fly me there for the weekend and then out to LA to see you afterwards if I wanted."

"Not to sway your decision, but we'd love to see you. We have to be careful of what Penelope is exposed to, but a nice remission celebration at home with a movie marathon and her favorite foods would be amazing."

Yes. It would. We both knew I couldn't afford the thousands of dollars a plane ticket would cost to come see her on my own. I reasoned if I was doing Reid the favor of accompanying him to the wedding, he could fly me out to California. My sister and I were prideful when it came to accepting charity, but this was more of an exchange of favors.

"I'll talk to him more about it tomorrow. But it would be nice to come home and visit. When is Penny's next doctor's appointment?"

She took the topic switch in stride. "In two weeks, she follows up with more blood tests. She's starting to get her energy back, so I'm optimistic it'll go well. Also, I have an interview on Friday. A real one. Hoping I can find a job with medical insurance."

God, I hoped so too because fighting cancer without insurance had been an absolute nightmare. It wasn't as if Tory hadn't done all she could to find a job with medical benefits, but starting work at a new company while taking time off for chemo appointments for a sick child had proved impossible. It was too bad my niece couldn't be on my medical insurance, but unfortunately, it didn't work that way.

"What's the job interview for?"

"An assistant position at a tech firm. If I can get a real job, I'm hoping to get a better apartment too."

They were in South Los Angeles, not in the best neighborhood. Someday we'd have a different life. One where I moved back and braided Penelope's newly grown hair, where we took her to a safe neighborhood park, and where we both didn't have to take off our clothes for strangers in order to fund cancer treatment for a child.

Someday.

"Did you quit your other job at the restaurant yet?"

I exhaled a large breath, not wanting to get into that. My "job" at the restaurant was a cover for stripping and doing so in a country where such activity was highly illegal. We couldn't mention it, not even over the phone. "Not yet. We can use the extra income to pay down the debt."

She shook her head, the annoyance obvious on her face over the ongoing argument between us. "I've got it covered, Teag. I mean it. Take your weekends off. You deserve it."

I was torn. On the one hand, I desperately wanted to quit stripping, especially given the risk here in the UAE, but on the other hand, the extra money would help us pay off the remaining medical debt and go toward getting a new apartment in a better neighborhood.

"We can put the money toward a new place."

One of the reasons I'd stayed past my one-year contract with Delmont Security was for the pay. The company covered my housing, and I was otherwise able to keep my costs low while making a decent wage. But if I was being truthful with myself, I wasn't sure I was ready to go home yet. I'd gotten a taste of adventure here in Dubai, and I selfishly didn't know if I was ready for it to end.

"I will sleep much better once you give notice, so please consider it. Good luck with your boss."

I'd need it. "Thanks. I'll be sending you lots of good vibes for your interview. Love you, sis."

She gave me one of her rare, genuine smiles. "Thanks. Love you too, Teag. Bye."

I hung up and sighed. For a girl who'd successfully avoided feelings for most of my life, it shouldn't be an issue to pretend I didn't have any when it came to Reid Maxwell and become his fake girlfriend. Right?

THE NEXT MORNING I was a ball of nerves when I knocked on

my boss's office door. I'd made up my mind. He wanted a fake girlfriend, and I was about to offer to play the part.

"Come in," came his deep-timbred voice.

He glanced up when I entered but then frowned when his phone rang. "Sorry, this will only take a moment if you don't mind waiting?"

"I don't mind."

It gave me a chance to observe him. Dammit. A crush consisted of pleasure, anxiety, hope, and hopelessness all at once. It was all-consuming, and not at all conducive to becoming his fake girlfriend. Then again, wouldn't it be nice to sit here without all of those feelings?

After hanging up his work call, he flashed me an apologetic smile. "Sorry to keep you waiting. What's up?"

I rubbed my palms against my black trousers. "Oh, um, you know, I thought I'd go with you to the wedding."

His brows jumped up. "No, no, like I said yesterday, I shouldn't have asked you to come with me."

"You're not asking. I'm offering."

An adorable blush stained his cheeks. "Why?"

Because I hoped to test my feelings for him. Either I'd get over my crush by getting to know him better, or I'd fall harder and get hurt. Win-win, right?

"First, I want to help you. Secondly, it would be a nice mini-vacation, and lastly, I intend to take you up on your offer to fly me to see my sister afterwards."

He seemed to contemplate. "You're not doing it because you feel sorry for my mopey ass?"

In reality, he had a fine ass, one I'd checked out more times than I could count. "No, although you should know I won't stand for any more mope. My fake boyfriends are quite happy to be with me."

He chuckled. "If I can't make a fake girlfriend fake happy, then what hope is there for me?"

"Exactly. So, how do you want to start stuff?"

"If you were serious about needing a gym buddy, then I'll take you up on the offer. You prefer mornings or evenings, after work?"

Seeing Reid in workout attire would be a treat. "As much as I hate mornings, I'd prefer to get a workout out of the way first thing."

"Tomorrow morning it is. I go to Eclipse a couple blocks away. Aiden introduced me to it."

It was a luxury gym, one way out of my salary band. "I'm not sure I'm an Eclipse kind of girl."

"Come on. I'll get you a pass. Since we'll have to pretend we've been dating, we can, uh, learn more about each other in the process."

My heart beat faster at the thought of spending time with him outside of work. "Okay. Yeah, we probably have a lot to learn in a short period." I might already have discovered a lot from stalking him over the last few months, but the truth was I didn't know what made Reid tick. I was looking forward to discovering more.

Chapter Six
REID

I'd never enjoyed the gym. But I had to admit getting out of bed with purpose for a change felt good this morning. This breakup had really messed with my head, but I was ready to put it behind me. That was why I'd put away the bottle of bourbon and decided I was done with nightly, numb-inducing drinking. No more.

Upon pulling into the gym parking lot, I spotted Teagan immediately. How could I not? She was tall and stunning. She had such a natural grace about her and an elegant way of moving. Like a dancer.

"Hi," I greeted, coming up from behind her and trying not to notice the way her yoga pants accentuated her muscular legs and amazing ass. *Jesus, focus.*

"Hi." She smiled, turning to give me my first glimpse of her T-shirt. "Crazy Ex-Girlfriend" was splashed across the front of it.

"Nice shirt."

She grinned. "I wear warning labels. Ready?"

"Let's do this."

Teagan was a firecracker. The type of woman who spoke

her mind and wasn't afraid to put anyone in their place if they stepped out of line. Not for the first time, I wondered what would happen when I took her to the wedding. Although I was friends with the groom and some of the fellow groomsmen, there'd be a lot of people who were the types I'd moved to the other side of the world to avoid.

We stepped into the gym, a spacious monstrosity consisting of multiple floors. Check-in was easy. It turned out I had complimentary passes for a guest with my membership.

"What's your torture?" I inquired, anticipating a good workout after which I'd need Motrin and a hot shower to ward off tomorrow's sore muscles.

She headed toward the fancy treadmills with televisions built into them. "I prefer to get the cardio out of the way first since I hate it the most."

Same. "Lead on."

She picked one machine while I took the one beside it. I should probably have stretched, but instead I focused on the way she was doing so. Side to side, she slipped easily into lunges, then held her knees up to her chest before rolling her neck and grabbing her arms behind her back.

"What's wrong?" she asked, cocking her head to the side.

Her question snapped me out of the dark rabbit hole of lusting after my assistant. Realizing I was staring, I shook my head. How had this happened? Maybe because I'd never seen her out of the work element. Or I could confess she had the longest, shapeliest legs I'd ever seen. The type made for wrapping around your waist and—

Nope. Not going there. Dammit. Maybe the gym had been a bad idea. "Nothing's wrong. Ready?"

I started off walking, the same as Teagan beside me, but when she switched to a jog, pride compelled me to do the same. Then she was running, and I was too, matching the nine on her speed despite knowing I'd regret it later. I was feeling good about myself until I realized she was at a five incline. Damn.

There came a time to admit defeat, but this wasn't it. Instead, I increased my incline. She merely raised a brow.

Later that afternoon in the office, I could already feel the effects of thirty minutes on the treadmill, during which I hadn't managed to keep up with my gym buddy. I'd also lifted free weights, and my arms were now remembering the familiar burn. I wasn't into fitness quite like my friend Aiden, but I definitely had missed pushing my body and doing something other than sitting on the couch.

Teagan came in with lunch at noon. Bye-bye, bacon cheeseburger, hello, salad.

"I got you a Cobb salad today. Don't worry, there's still bacon, but no onions since you dislike them."

"How did you know?"

She shrugged. "Um, the one time I suggested onion rings instead of fries you might have told me."

Made sense. "You want to have lunch in here? We can talk game plan over the next two weeks."

"Sure, let me grab my sandwich. I'll be back."

We ate in silence for ten minutes before I broached my plan. I didn't want to freak her out, but I'd been preparing extensively. It was my nature as I was a planner.

"I'll book your flight today if you're okay with it. I figured we can fly out the previous Thursday morning. With the time difference, we arrive the same day in the afternoon. Then on Sunday, the day after the wedding, you can fly to LA. How long do you want to stay there?"

"Returning the next Friday will give me almost a week there. Thank you for flying me out to LA. My sister and niece are excited about it."

I made a note in my planner. "Got it. So this morning, due to me being embarrassingly out of shape, and breathing heavily, we didn't get to discuss our backgrounds. For people to believe we're serious, we should discuss our families and history."

Her brow lifted. "We're serious? In your scenario?"

"As serious as a couple of months of dating can be, but we could go with the 'we've been friends over the last year and it turned into more after the breakup.'" I didn't want people to think she was a rebound as it would undermine the entire plan. "I suppose we could start with what you already know about me."

She hesitated before beginning. "I know you're originally from New Hampshire. Is Vanessa from your hometown too?"

"Yes."

She chuckled. "Okay, big talker, this may take a while if we do yes and no answers."

"Sorry, but I'm not big on talking about my ex." I was suddenly embarrassed to share my history with Vanessa.

"I get it, but if she'll be at the wedding, I need the five-cent rundown, so I'm armed appropriately."

"Armed is an interesting choice of words. And probably accurate given the people who will be there. It's bound to be awkward for you." It was only fair I warn her.

She shrugged, apparently not at all concerned. "Awkward is cake. Now lay the history on me."

"Okay. I met Vanessa in sixth grade when her family moved to town, but we didn't start dating until we were in college. I went to Harvard, and she was at Boston University. Since we were close, we'd often see each other at parties or amongst mutual friends."

All through grade school and high school I'd had a thing for her, but she hadn't noticed me until my freshman year of college when I'd returned home during a Christmas vacation. Of course, it helped I'd shot up four inches and filled out by then.

God, I'd been so infatuated with her at the time. Our relationship had been easy at first, but then once I'd finished grad school, and we began discussing a post-college relationship, we'd disagreed about everything from where we'd live, where I'd work, and what our future plans would hold.

No matter how much I'd loved her, it wasn't in me to take advantage of family ties and go to work for her father in Boston as she'd desired. I didn't want to live in a world of trust funds and lavish country club parties or even stay in my hometown. I needed to earn my own way. Make my own mark. In hindsight, it was no wonder we'd broken up so often. We'd never wanted the same things for our future.

Teagan seemed to read my mind. "You mentioned you broke up a few times?"

I expelled a frustrated breath. "Yeah. Typically the breakups were short-lived, but after undergrad, we were apart for nearly a year." She'd gone off to Paris, and I dated someone I'd met in my apartment building. But then Vanessa had returned saying Paris had changed her, and she'd missed me and wanted a reconciliation. I'd hurt Shelly by going back to Vanessa. It was a lesson to never start another rebound relationship, because hurting someone was the last thing I wished to do again.

"Did you assume you'd reconcile each time you broke up?"

My hand went to the back of my neck in a gesture of discomfort over this conversation. Honestly, my entire relationship had been a roller coaster, one I wasn't proud I had ridden time and time again. Unfortunately, I'd put Vanessa in control over the majority of our time together.

"I didn't always believe we'd reconcile, but it became our unhealthy pattern. A year ago, before I left for Dubai, I believed we'd broken up for good, especially since I'd taken this job so far away. Then she came out here, and we reconciled. Things seemed better, and we got engaged. The plan was for her to move here until I finished my contract, and then I'd transfer to Delmont Security's New York office, where we'd make our lives." Manhattan had been the compromise to keep her close enough to her family and me far enough from mine.

"How did you go from broken up to engaged?"

"Because I was an idiot" was the short answer. "When she declared she was ready to start a life together and proposed marriage, I believed she was serious and would move to Dubai to be with me. But then it was one excuse after another as to why she wouldn't join me. Ultimately, she didn't want to leave her life behind. Then she cheated, and you know the rest."

"Wait, she proposed to you?"

"Technically, yes. But then I bought her the ring. Anyhow, enough of the history recap. If I were actually dating you, I'm not sure I would've shared that much."

It felt awkward as hell to reveal the details about my relationship with Vanessa. Staying with her as long as I had painted me as pathetic. It had been a mistake to believe she'd loved me enough to let go of her privileged roots and live a life outside of her safety bubble.

"Okay, we'll nix the ex talk for now."

Thank God. "Okay, your turn. What do I need to know about your past? Begin with your family."

Her eyes widened slightly before she forced a shrug. "My sister is four years older than me. She lives in Los Angeles with my niece."

"What about your parents?"

She exhaled a shaky breath. "I never knew my father. And my mom took off when I was thirteen. I went through foster care for a year until my sister became an adult and my legal guardian. Dropped out of high school my junior year, but I got my GED."

I swallowed hard. There was an edge I'd always noticed in Teagan, and I had no doubt her harsh upbringing had contributed to it. The pain in her eyes made it clear she didn't want to talk about it.

She fidgeted with the silver bracelet on her left wrist. "It's not exactly the type of background you want for your fake girlfriend at a wedding. I get it."

I didn't give a fuck what people thought of her background. But I didn't want her to have to feel defensive among the bunch of pretentious assholes I knew would be at the wedding.

"You can tell them whatever you want about your past. Make up something for all I care."

Chapter Seven
TEAGAN

In other words, I should invent a background story and family history worthy of Reid's friends and family and not as embarrassing as the truth.

It stung, but it shouldn't. He was bringing me to a wedding with his affluent friends and family to prove he'd moved on with someone better, not to show that he'd downgraded. He'd been engaged to the belle of the ball. He couldn't now be dating a meth head's daughter whose sperm donor father could've been any one of the men with whom my mother had traded sexual favors for drugs.

Old insecurities hit me from a place I'd shoved them years ago. But I forced a smile. During my adult life, I'd grown used to putting on a show. I pretended my crappy childhood hadn't affected me. Pretended I was over the trauma of my unstable upbringing, and most of all, I pretended I didn't give a shit about anyone else's opinion of me. There might not be any awards in my future, but I'd certainly perfected the act of not caring.

"I'll say I'm from Los Angeles, went to college at UCLA,

and if anyone asks about my family, I'll tell them both my parents died when I was younger."

I hated the sympathy reflected in his eyes.

"Whatever you feel comfortable saying."

"We should go with that. Probably also shouldn't mention I'm your assistant."

He sighed. "I guess I'd hate for someone to wonder if I'm taking advantage. We'll say we work together. Maybe you work in another department."

"Right. I could be a manager in another department. Gives a better impression than if I were only an assistant or an analyst."

His brow furrowed. "I don't think going that far is necessary—"

"No, it's fine." I preferred to present the best possible scenario for Reid. But I'd be lying if I said it didn't kill me a little inside to realize that even if he reciprocated my feelings, there was no way we could ever be together. Not given my background, not to mention my current illegal stripping job.

Remember, Teagan. You're Cheese Whiz.

"What did you do in LA before moving here?"

"Nothing important."

After obtaining my GED, I'd started attending community college but found little interest in academics. I'd worked a number of odd jobs until cosmetology had piqued my interest, and I'd started taking some classes. But once my niece was born and my sister had needed help, I'd pushed it off. Then, of course, there had been the diagnosis, which had forced us both into desperate measures. I'd begun stripping in LA, but it became apparent it wasn't earning enough. So when I'd been offered the opportunity to work for Delmont Security in Dubai, I'd jumped at it. To my relief, I'd then discovered the club, The Scarlet Letter, where I'd be able to earn two thousand dollars a week for taking off my clothes and dancing.

Reid was frowning. "I consider anything about you important. What did you do?"

Leave it to him to show kindness. "I worked some odds jobs before going to cosmetology school, but I didn't finish. I wasn't much on regular classes, but I loved the idea of skin care, makeup and hair. But I think it's best we stick with the story I gave you instead of the truth. Let's say I'm in accounting." Seemed like a safe, non-question-inducing vocation.

He hesitated but finally seemed to sense my desire to drop the subject. "Okay. Accounting it is. Will you wear glasses? Crunch some numbers?"

My grin came easily. "Why, Reid Maxwell, do you have some secret fantasies about accountants you've been hiding?"

His cheeks went pink, but the amusement was evident in his eyes. "It's the calculator that does it for me. Will you start wearing glasses? Maybe put a pencil behind your ear?"

His flirtatious side was unexpected and fun. "For you, I'll even throw in a messy bun and a pencil skirt."

He cleared his voice and glanced down at his calendar. "So, what's your schedule over the next couple weeks?"

"You asking me out?" Could I help teasing him a bit? His deeper blush made it worth it.

"I figured we need to spend time together, but if you don't want to—"

"Of course I want to." Jesus, anxious much? I needed to tone this down before I scared him off. "In order to make this believable, hanging out is the best way to get to know each other, and get more comfortable."

"Makes sense. What's your weekend look like?"

In Dubai, the work week was Sunday through Thursday, with Friday and Saturday as the weekend. But I worked on

Thursday and Friday nights at the "restaurant." "I have to work both nights, but I'm free during the days."

"I forgot that Aiden mentioned you worked with Chloe at a restaurant nearby. Will it be a problem getting the weekend off for the wedding?"

"No, not at all." The club was flexible with scheduling.

"Great. Let's pencil in some time together."

Chapter Eight

TEAGAN

Stripping wasn't something I enjoyed, but I'd always been a good dancer, so it came quite naturally. But even I'd had to up my game when it came to dancing at the Scarlett Letter. There were a number of women from all over the world working there, many of whom were beyond striking and could work a pole as though their lives depended on it. Considering the entry fee was ten grand, and it cost five hundred for ten minutes in the back room, we had to perform at a high caliber for the rich men who came into the place.

I didn't make friends at the club—other than Chloe, who I'd known before bringing her in. None of us got cozy with each other. It was better that way given we were all breaking the law in a foreign country. We all had our reasons for taking the risk. Some of the women had worked here only a few months, others had been doing it a year or more. There were only a handful of times the club had been shut down because of the possible risk of discovery, but it was always a threat.

It was rumored the club was funded by someone in the royal family, but I'd heard it also had American ties.

There were some regulars, but mostly we had rich men

who came in groups from out of town. To protect our identities, we wore masks. In addition, I donned a long red wig to cover my hair. It was easier than arranging my hair every night, and it also lent to my stage name of Ruby.

Going into the club later that night was a somber affair. I wasn't ever overly excited to go strip, but at least when Chloe had been here, we'd been in it together and could picture the McDonald's run at the end of the evening. She had an obsession with cheeseburgers, and I could hoover a Big Mac and large fries any day.

Some nights were better than others. This Friday night wasn't one of the better ones.

"No touching on the floor, sir," I said for the second time while giving a suit a lap dance.

My eyes hit those of the nearest bouncer. He was a large, scary man, ready to pounce if I flashed the signal.

The stranger's hot, tequila-infused breath hit my ear, making me shiver from disgust. "Let's go to a room."

I had a rule about working the rooms in the back, a pact Chloe and I had made while she'd worked here with me. But the thought of the extra money was hard to pass up. The sooner I earned the cash to pay the sixty grand owed in medical debt and save for a better apartment for my niece and sister, the sooner I could quit this job.

What was the worst that could happen? There were cameras in the room, and I got to call the shots.

"Let's go." I stood up, about to lead him to the private rooms. But suddenly Reid's face came to mind.

I shook my head, trying to ditch the thought from my head. Although I'd been crushing on my boss for almost a year, he'd never entered my brain while I was at the club. It was as though I had a hard limit against inviting the two ideas together. But now we'd been spending so much more time in each other's company.

Before work, we'd been meeting at the gym every day. Though we mostly did our own things, it turned out becoming gym buddies was not exactly quelling my crush. If anything, it was intensifying it.

And if I'd needed a reminder of why it couldn't go beyond a crush, all I had to do was look down at the meaty paw grasping my wrist as though I was his new plaything. The man's grip was a cruel reminder I was just a stripper and definitely not girlfriend material. Shit. Bringing this stranger back to a private room had been a mistake. I wasn't in the right head space.

But it was too late now. I'd give him a spectacular private dance, and hopefully then he'd be on his way.

As soon as we entered the room, however, the man with a thick Russian accent was on me. A tongue was shoved into my mouth, and I nearly choked on the taste of tequila and cigar smoke.

"No," I shouted, trying to pull away. But he wasn't having it. I flashed the peace sign, the club's signal for distress and hoped the cameras weren't just for show.

Finally, I was able to jerk away, my lungs heaving hard at the assault, but I didn't want to cause a scene. Although the bouncers were here to protect the girls, I had to remember customer service always came first. To the club, money was king.

"There's no kissing."

"Bullshit. I pay. I want whore."

"Sir, I'm afraid you misunderstand—" I didn't see the hand fly toward my face until it was too late.

Holy shit, he'd slapped me. The tang of blood hit my mouth at the same time the bouncers came through the door.

Bouncer number one, known as Toby—short for something the girls here couldn't pronounce—said, "Come with me, sir, and we can see to your needs."

For the right price, they'd probably take him next door to the hotel where they ran an escort service. The thought of some poor girl, probably even more desperate than I was for money, getting slapped around by this man all night made me sick to my stomach.

Luckily, the suit followed Toby out the door without protest, leaving me with Rahoul. He was a large, burly man who hardly spoke a word but carried a large knife strapped to his thigh. "You okay?"

My palm pressed against my throbbing jaw. "I think so."

"Go take ten minutes and put makeup on to cover it, then return to the floor."

He didn't give me an opportunity to ask for more than the ten minutes offered. This was a business. And I was a commodity. Period.

The next morning I woke up with black and blue dotting my jaw. The blood had come from me biting my tongue, which was the silver lining since I didn't have a cut lip. But the incident left me shaken. I had the next weekend off for the wedding, but there was no doubt now. I wanted to quit.

I'd search for a legitimate second job once I returned from seeing my sister in Los Angeles. My niece was in remission, and although it might take years to pay down the debt and save up for a better apartment, I needed to get out of stripping. My sister had already said she'd understand.

Then why was I crying? Maybe because last night had reminded me of exactly how I was valued in society. As a meth head's daughter. As a foster kid. As a high school dropout. As a stripper. As Cheese Whiz.

I sucked in a deep breath. Per usual, my insecurities

circled back to Reid. Dammit. Agreeing to become his fake girlfriend was messing with my head. It called attention to the ways I was lacking, and all the reasons I could never be his real girlfriend. This was the problem with thinking for a moment my crush could ever be anything more.

It was time for a new plan. A plan to put this crush behind me once and for all.

Chapter Nine

REID

Teagan and I continued hitting the gym together despite how awkward I felt about my unexpected attraction to her. Stupidly, I couldn't manage to verbalize that maybe it was too intimate to be sweating together each morning.

I did make a point to do my workout separately from hers. That way I absolutely did not stare at her ass. Or notice her long legs. Or stalk her with my eyes across the gym when she'd change machines.

Much.

I reasoned it was normal and harmless to be attracted to a beautiful woman. Hell, maybe it was a good thing, as I could practice flexing my flirting muscles with a woman who was safely in the friend zone before getting back out there into dating waters.

At least she ensured I went every morning. After only five days of eating healthy and going to the gym, I dropped a couple pounds and also started sleeping again. I no longer felt bloated or lacked energy. My body had detoxed from the heavy drinking and junk food, and I was finally feeling back to my old self.

I'd enjoyed learning more about Teagan over the last few days too. I'd learned her favorite color was blue, she didn't wear pink because it clashed with her red hair, she loved seafood, especially sushi, hated Brussels sprouts with the power of a thousand suns—her words—and had a weakness for cinnamon rolls.

She also loved anything caramel, which would include the caramel macchiato I'd picked up before her arrival at my apartment Saturday morning.

After opening the door to her knock, I found myself temporarily speechless.

"Hi," she greeted. Her hair was twisted up in a top bun, and she was dressed casually in a T-shirt and shorts. Although I'd always thought she was beautiful, seeing her fresh-faced in my doorframe was causing an unexpected shot of lust.

"Can I come in?"

"Yes. Of course." I moved aside, allowing her to step into my apartment.

My eyes wandered down to see today's T-shirt displayed, "I like coffee and maybe three people."

My chuckle came easily. "If I give you coffee, does it mean I'm one of the three people you like?"

Her gaze landed on the cup sitting on my kitchen counter. "Is that a caramel macchiato?"

"It is indeed."

She frowned.

"I'm sorry. I thought it was your favorite."

Her face turned pink. "No, it is. I'm the one who's sorry because my mind just spaced. Thank you. You've made the short list of three, and are the best fake boyfriend ever."

Funny how when I'd been a real boyfriend I'd hardly

received the same amount of appreciation. "You're welcome."

I was about to suggest she take a seat at my kitchen table when I noticed the bruise. Lifting my hand up to her face, I laid my fingers along her jaw. I didn't even realize I'd done so until her eyes went wide at the contact. I quickly dropped my hand. "What happened?"

"Nothing. Just a stupid boxing workout class yesterday. The girl next to me got too close."

I had no reason to doubt her as it was plausible she'd taken a workout class on her own, and yet I found myself unconvinced. "You okay?"

"Yeah, yeah. It's fine. But obviously my makeup skills need help." She sipped on her drink and looked around the place. "So this is your apartment. Nice."

It was decent, albeit boring, with its white walls and gray modern furniture. But at least as an executive I had my own apartment, unlike Teagan. "Thanks. You prefer to sit at my kitchen table or in the living room?"

She bypassed the quaint table and went for the couch. "This is more comfortable."

Having her in my space was anything but comfortable. I wasn't sure why. "How was work last night?" A lot of the staff who accepted contracts to work in Dubai for a year also worked second jobs for extra money, so I wasn't surprised Teagan had chosen that route too.

But Teagan hesitated in answering my simple question, making me wonder.

"It was fine. It'll be nice to have next weekend off."

"Why don't you give me the name of the place? Always up for trying new things." Never was there a falser statement. I was a creature of habit. But suddenly I was curious to find out where she spent her weekend hours.

"I may be switching restaurants, but I'll let you know where I land. You could come in then."

The timing of her bruise and change of job set off alarm bells. Was it possible she'd been involved in some type of altercation at work? Whatever had happened, it was clear she wasn't ready to share it, and I hadn't meant to make her uneasy with the topic.

I switched tacks. "I'm curious. Your year-long contract has been up for three months, correct?"

"Yeah, but I extended for six months."

Which meant she had three months remaining. "Why?" Most people left after their year was up.

She played with her straw. "I enjoy my job here."

"You don't miss LA?"

"I miss my sister and niece, but I'll move back eventually."

If it was the money keeping her here, it was clear she didn't want to talk about it. Her attitude reminded me to insist on paying for her clothes and anything else she'd need for the trip. I absolutely didn't want to burden her with any expense in doing me this favor.

"What about you? How long will you stay in Dubai?" she queried.

"I signed on for a two-year contract." I was sixteen months into it now.

"After your contract is up, do you think you'll go to New York as you originally planned?"

I shook my head. "Definitely not. I applied for another job in Delmont's Sydney office." I'd put in for the promotion the regional director had recommended. Australia sounded like a great place to live for a couple of years. Rumor had it the women there were knockouts, so perhaps it was the perfect place to enjoy a single life and have a fresh start. "As far as what we tell people at the wedding, let's say we plan on staying in Dubai for now."

She chewed on her bottom lip. "Makes sense. I've heard wonderful things about Australia. I bet you'll enjoy it."

"I still need to get the job. But I've heard good things too. So, I thought we'd go over our favorite movies and music today."

She smirked. "Did you make a list of things we need to find out about each other before we leave for the wedding?"

My face heated. "I like to stay organized."

"Which is admirable, but we may want to go about it more organically, so it doesn't seem rehearsed."

She had a point. The fifty questions might seem too practiced. "What do you suggest?"

"Deeper conversation."

"Like what?"

She contemplated while I felt the buzz of my phone.

I took it out and looked at the screen but didn't recognize the number. It appeared to be from overseas. "I'm sorry. Do you mind if I take this? It might be Aiden."

"No, I don't mind at all."

I stood up and walked to the kitchen to answer the phone, hoping it was my best friend. He was in Iraq now as a government contractor, so I worried about him and hoped he was keeping safe. "Hello."

"Hi, it's Aiden."

I blew out a breath of relief. Hearing his voice meant he remained in one piece. Considering he'd signed on for a dangerous assignment in a war zone, was there any wonder I worried? "How are you? You doing okay?"

"I'm doing all right. Still in Iraq. It's a shit show here, nothing close to the military, for sure. I could use your help in a personal matter."

My eyes immediately fell on Teagan sitting on the couch. "Of course. What can I do?"

"I'm leaving next week and heading to LA to see Chloe. I want to surprise her. But to do it right, I need her friend Kendall's contact information. Chloe is currently staying at her place."

"You're in luck. Teagan is here now. Let me ask her for it."

"Teagan is with you now? I'd love to hear that story." He chuckled.

"Rain check on that." I turned to see Teagan now standing, her head cocked to the side at the mention of her name.

"Aiden wants to know if you have Kendall's contact information. He's trying to plan a surprise for Chloe."

Her gaze narrowed, and she held out her hand for the phone.

Amused, I walked over to let her take it.

"Hi, Aiden, this is Teagan. Explain to me why the hell I should help you after you broke my best friend's heart."

She stood quietly, listening to whatever Aiden was saying to her. Then suddenly she pulled out her phone, seemingly searching for something. "All right, you've convinced me. For now. But know that I have high expectations you will grovel properly once you get to LA and see Chloe. And of course, I fully expect you to make her deliriously happy."

I couldn't hear what my best friend was saying, but from the way Teagan had relented about giving him the information, I assumed he must've been persuasive. After reciting the details, she handed my phone back to me with a smile.

"You have what you need?" I asked Aiden and heard him chuckle in response.

"I do. To be honest, I feel safer here in Iraq than I will if I screw this up with Chloe and Teagan finds out."

Now it was my turn to laugh. "I'd say your assessment is fair. Be safe this next week, so you can get to LA. Okay?" He'd already lost half a leg to the war; I certainly didn't want him to sacrifice anything else—like his life.

"Will do. We'll talk again soon."

"Yeah, soon. Goodbye."

"Bye."

I hung up, my eyes fixed on the fiery redhead in front of me. "I don't think I've ever seen anyone put Aiden on the spot the way you did."

She shrugged. "Wasn't as if I was about to give him the address and say feel free to go break Chloe's heart again."

"He must've been pretty convincing."

She rolled her eyes. "He wasn't bad. I just hope he follows through. She loves him."

"He loves her too. But he was too stubborn to realize he was worthy of her. Sounds as though he's come to his senses."

"We'll see."

"Mm, sounds cynical?"

She sat back on the couch and tucked her long legs beneath her. "I'm not cynical, just wary."

"Why?"

She sighed, clearly not wanting to talk about this subject.

"You're the one who suggested deeper conversation."

"Yeah, but more like what is your favorite memory as a child?"

"My favorite memory is from when I was eight years old. It was the summer we went up on a family vacation to Maine. Aiden's family went with us, and I spent all three weeks swimming, fishing, and running around with my best friend and my older brother. That's my favorite memory from childhood. Now then, why are you so wary? Bad relationship?"

Chapter Ten

TEAGAN

When I'd suggested we have deeper conversation, I'd meant about him. If I was to get over this crush, then I needed to know more than his favorite color. It was orange, by the way. Whose favorite color was orange? It was the color my nightmares were made of, a color I'd never be caught dead wearing with my red hair.

Yet despite learning his poor favorite color choice, my crush was far from abating. Especially when he had to go do something thoughtful like get me my favorite coffee drink. Therefore I was actively hunting for a deal-breaker. The one thing that would be an instant turnoff and rid me of my feelings once and for all.

He took a seat next to me on the couch, his nearness doing funny things to my insides. "Tell me why you're so wary."

I decided to be honest, curious as to what type of reaction it would illicit on his part. "My mother was a meth addict. She was always making promises she didn't keep. Same thing went for anyone else she brought around. So over the years, it became harder for people to earn my confidence." I didn't mention my high school boyfriend who'd crushed all my teenage hopes by telling me I wasn't good enough for him or his rich family.

Reid visibly swallowed. "What about your sister? Is she someone you trust?"

"Always. Tory was always there for me growing up. We're close."

"And your niece is how old now?"

"She's four. She was quite sick this past year with leukemia."

His eyes went wide. "Christ. Did she beat it?"

"So far, it appears so. She's the bravest person I know." I hadn't meant to share so much, yet Reid was easy to talk to. "So that's as deep as I go. Now then, what's your favorite kind of music?"

His grin was contagious. "Ah, all of a sudden my list is appealing again?"

It was indeed. The surface stuff was safer. And who knew? Maybe I'd find out he loved country music, and my crush would go poof, gone. "How about we compromise and do one deep conversation per day?"

"Deal. And I'm fond of jazz music."

I crinkled my nose. Jazz was even worse than country. "But you're under sixty—how is that possible?"

He chuckled. "It's possible because I have an appreciation for real music. I also love classical. None of this pop rap crap."

"You do realize pop and rap are two different types of music?"

"Most of them meld together these days. And have you ever listened to jazz? Real jazz from a vinyl record?"

His unapologetic love for his horrible taste in music was sexy. Dammit.

"How old are you again?" I teased.

He grinned. "Thirty-two. Thirty-three on September tenth. When is your birthday?"

"September ninth if you can believe it." I'd always thought it was funny our birthdays were one day apart. "But of course, I'm eight years younger."

"Only seven years on September the ninth."

"And who says one day doesn't make a difference?" I joked. "Okay, now we know we'll never agree on music because I love pop, let's talk movies. What are your favorite types?"

"All types really. Of course I like action flicks, but I prefer the black-and-white classics."

"And now I'm convinced you're older than you look."

He shrugged. "I have an old spirit. And they don't make movies like they did back in the day, I promise you. Matter of fact, if we were actually dating, I'd make you come over and watch one and listen to jazz music."

"If we were actually dating, I might pretend I was excited about a black-and-white movie and old-person music."

He chuckled. "No, you wouldn't."

I joined in his laughter. "You're right, I totally wouldn't." Instead I'd give him a hard time just as I was now.

His face suddenly took on a serious expression. "I've had a lot of fun these last few days."

"The gym is your idea of fun?"

"No, but hanging out during our work lunches has been."

My eyes pricked with tears from the pang of longing which suddenly hit me. For a moment I could picture truly falling for him. I pushed to my feet, walking over to take in the view from his window to keep him from seeing my stupid, unexpected emotion. "Hanging out with you has been fun too," I said. "Are you hungry?"

"Yeah. We could do a light lunch, then maybe something bigger for dinner?"

"Lunch and dinner?" I turned to face him. Were we spending the entire day together?

He got up off the couch and strode into the kitchen. "Sorry, I'm being presumptuous. You probably have other plans."

"You're looking at them. I have to say it's been quite boring without Chloe. My apartment feels empty, so it's nice to get out."

"When will they assign you another roommate?"

"It could be any day."

I hoped whoever they placed with me was laid-back and sweet like Chloe had been. I was the type of girl you either hated or loved. There was no in between. My "extra," as people called it, was definitely an acquired taste. I tended to get overly excited about mundane things and overly sensitive about other things. When I was a child, the teachers had called it ADD, but as an adult, I preferred to think of it as having a lot of enthusiasm.

Reid pulled takeout menus out of a kitchen drawer and walked over to hand me a few. "As you can see, I have quite the pick of restaurants who deliver."

The thought of spending an entire day with him had me giddy. But this wouldn't do. I had to dig a little deeper into Reid Maxwell and hope for a disgusting habit or some other turnoff. Hadn't my sister said the quickest way to rid me of my crush was to really get to know the man?

I decided on my next round of questions over a lunch of turkey sandwiches and tomato soup.

"Was Vanessa your first time?" That would've meant he'd waited until college, but I could see him holding out for her.

His adorable face turned the same color of the soup. "No, she wasn't."

"Anyone else you were ever serious about?"

He sighed. "Is this relevant to our fake relationship?"

No, but I wanted the details for my own selfish get-over-my-crush reasons. "Definitely. I'd want the details of who you've ever been involved with."

"Fine. There were a few others when we were on breaks."

Interesting. "Anyone serious?"

Another long, exasperated breath. "For me, no. For one of them, a little bit. I don't enjoy talking about this."

I suddenly had a clear picture. "You dated someone while on a break, she fell for you, but you were still in love with Vanessa and got back together with her."

"I'm not proud of it. That's why this"—he motioned between us—"is so much better. The last thing I want to do is hurt anyone or risk another rebound relationship."

"Is there a chance you'd take Vanessa back?"

His jaw clenched. "No. Not this time."

"Because she cheated on you?"

"Yes."

I wondered if it had been a long-term affair for Vanessa or only a single night. "Was your brother into her over the years?"

He shook his head. "No. Quite the opposite. She crushed on him in high school, but all the girls did. He was cool while all the other teenagers were awkward. Anyhow, he didn't pay Vanessa any attention. In fact, when I got together with her, he was vocal about his displeasure with it. Ironically, he'd warned me she might cheat. Then he turned out to be the one she cheated with. Anyways, how did we end up rehashing this tired subject?"

"Guess I had some residual questions."

"How about you? Who was your first time?"

It wasn't relevant to our whole fake dating scheme, but I thought it was only fair to reciprocate. "Johnny Mills in tenth grade. I was rebelling, and it was nothing worth remembering except that it was my first."

"Anyone serious for you?"

I shook my head. "Nope. I had a high school boyfriend for, like, three months." Before I'd realized he was too ashamed of me to tell people we were dating. "Guess I'm not one for commitment." Because commitment meant trusting someone wouldn't leave. It meant being vulnerable. And it meant there was a good chance they'd let you down in the end.

"See? One more reason this arrangement is perfect."

Right. Because he wouldn't have to worry about me getting attached. My eyes wandered around his apartment, looking for a lifeline, anything to change the subject. "Is that a game controller?" I could see it under his television and was instantly curious. But I was even more surprised by the way he reacted.

He jumped up as if the discovery was offensive and quickly shoved the device into a drawer.

I caught a glimpse of a gaming system before he got the drawer shut again. "Do you have an Xbox?"

He turned, his face red. "Yeah, but I don't play it. Much."

"Right. You just leave the controller out." I was up and pulling the drawer open before he could stop me. In it was an Xbox, a headset, and two controllers. When I opened another drawer, it revealed a number of games.

"Anyone ever tell you you're extremely nosey?"

I threw a grin over my shoulder. "All the time. Care to revise your earlier statement about not playing much?"

His face was still red. "It's to kill the solitude, ya know."

I took out two controllers. "I do know. Now pick your poison. Which game should we play?"

He stared at me. "You want to play?"

"I'd love to." I'd always wanted a video game system while growing up, but it was a luxury we couldn't afford. "I may not be very good."

He seemed to relax. "I'll teach you."

I decided to let go of my mission to find a turnoff and just give in to the moment. Getting over my crush would have to wait for another day, because discovering this secret side of Reid was definitely not doing it.

Two hours later we'd gone through all of Mortal Kombat, and currently I was getting my ass kicked in some kind of survival game. We spent the entire afternoon laughing while he taught me all the moves and tricks of the games. "Sure, you hardly play. You're a gamer, Reid Maxwell."

His adorable face heated yet again, making me put the controller aside.

"Yet, you're weirdly embarrassed about it. Why?"

Chapter Eleven

REID

I was embarrassed about being embarrassed about being called out, even though I had nothing to be ashamed of. I'm sure if you surveyed most men, they'd owned a video game system at some point in their life. Teagan wasn't wrong. I was a gamer. I'd been gaming since I received my first PlayStation for Christmas when I was six years old. I'd cut my teeth on Mortal Kombat 3 and had enjoyed gaming ever since.

"Come on. Deeper conversation, remember?"

"Thought you said we were limiting it to one per day?"

She shrugged. "Let's go for two, and you get tomorrow out of the way early."

Why not? Teagan had already dealt with me at my worst. She'd staged an intervention for my excessive drinking and general mopeyness and then offered to play my fake girlfriend because I was too much of a pussy to go to a wedding alone. So what was one more admission to seal the deal?

"Fine. I was introverted as a kid. While my parents were married, they argued constantly, and video games were my escape. My brother used to play with me." Hell, over the last decade, despite our busy schedules and hellishly different time zones, we'd made a point to meet up for a monthly game. Thinking about it reminded me of how much I missed it now.

"Anyhow, I kept playing, but it became a lot less cool as I got older."

"I take it the ex didn't enjoy playing games with you?"

Oh, she enjoyed playing games, all right, but not this type. "She abhorred video games or anything which took the attention away from her."

"So you got used to hiding it."

Indeed I had. In the same way, I'd pretended to be a lot of things in order to be more or less for Vanessa over the years. "I did."

"Any chance you have Mario Kart Racing?"

Playing with Teagan over the last hour had been more fun than I could remember having in a long time. Although she hadn't been great, her enthusiasm for gaming was contagious. The way she approached everything with wide-eyed wonder reminded me of myself as a kid.

"Afraid I don't have Mario Kart, but I could pick it up." I'd have to purchase a Nintendo gaming system while I was at it, but I definitely didn't mind if it meant we could play again.

"Cool. Maybe it would be something I don't suck at."

She stood up, and so did I.

She suddenly cocked her head to the side as if something had dawned on her. "Should we practice kissing?"

"What?"

"Kissing. You know, to make it appear natural."

Dammit, I could feel my face heat. And when she stepped closer, I couldn't help sucking in a breath and widening my eyes.

She burst out laughing. "See, that's what you can't do. You can't stare at me like, 'what the hell are you doing?' Instead, try to convey a look of 'I don't freak out at the thought of kissing you.'"

I cleared my throat, awkward about this entire situation. "Okay, I'll work on it. Maybe it's because kissing a friend doesn't feel entirely natural."

She smirked. "No, I don't suppose it is."

"We'll be dancing at the wedding reception, so maybe that's a good place to practice, you know, touching each other. Dance with me?"

"Sure."

I took her into my arms, dancing her around the living room. I was happy I'd had lessons, so I didn't embarrass myself. She was stiff at first but then finally relaxed.

But after a while, she started giggling and shaking her head.

"What?"

"This is formal dancing. But dancing with someone you are in love with or at least you've had sex with should be closer, more intimate."

I swallowed hard, especially at her mention of sex. Since she was so tall, she was only a few inches shorter than my six foot two. I slowed it down as if I was dancing with a lover. "You'll be near my height when you're wearing heels."

"Does it bother you?"

"Not at all." I appreciated the way she fit my body. A little too much if I was being honest.

"Good. Put your hands on my ass."

I could not have heard her correctly. "Pardon?"

"I said, put your hands on my ass."

Chapter Twelve
TEAGAN

After I repeated my words, Reid stepped back as if I'd asked him to kick a kitten. "Absolutely not."

What could I say? I hadn't been able to help myself. I wanted to push boundaries with him. Besides, if I learned he was a prude or terrible at kissing, I would no longer be attracted to him. "Come on. It doesn't have to be a groping session. Just a little wicked promise for all to see."

He took my arms and returned to dance mode, shaking his head. "I'm not grabbing your ass on the dance floor at a wedding reception in front of family and friends."

"Come on, it's not like I'm asking you to hump my leg. We're talking a sexy skim." God, it was fun pushing him out of his comfort zone.

He rolled his eyes. "I'm not much for PDA."

"So you weren't affectionate with the ex?"

He led me in a slow circle as if to the beat of his own music. "No. She didn't care for it. Always thought PDA was tacky."

"Mm." I was beginning to get a clearer picture of Vanessa. And it wasn't a favorable one. I mean for God's sake, the man had to hide video games from her? Did she have a list of rules for him to follow in bed too?

He leaned back to study my face. "No. Get the gleam out of your eye."

I feigned innocence. "I don't have a gleam."

He chuckled. "Fine, we'll label it a twinkle, then. But get the idea out of your head."

"Hear me out. I just think if she's not used to seeing you act physically affectionate, it would send a message to see you grab my ass."

"What is with you wanting me to grab your ass?"

"Hey, you say that as if you don't appreciate this ass. I work hard for it. I believe any fake boyfriend of mine would be anxious to, you know, touch it."

He was already shaking his head, a wide smile on his face. "I'll take it under advisement, but we should probably walk before we run."

"Meaning you're ready to kiss me now?" With any luck, it would be terrible and burst my crush bubble once and for all.

He stopped dancing, his face taking on a serious expression. "Yeah, I suppose we should get to it."

Oh, boy. Suddenly all humor between us faded. While my mouth went dry, my palms started to sweat. This was it. This was the instant I would no longer adore Reid Maxwell.

But when his hands framed my face, and he leaned forward, I freaked the fuck out. There was no other way to describe it.

In a combination of blowing out my breath in his face and stepping back so awkwardly I tripped over my own feet, I committed the ultimate embarrassment of landing on my ass.

"Jesus, what the hell happened?" He reached down to help me up.

"I don't entirely know." I totally knew.

"Are you okay?" Concern was etched on his face.

"Fine. Um, I just remembered I have to be somewhere."

"What? Where? I thought we were doing dinner?"

I was already across the room, gathering my purse and halfway to the door. "I realized I'm late for a thing. But we can do this again sometime. Bye."

Adrenaline fueled my escape from his apartment, taking me to the elevator where I pressed the down button no less than ten times.

I was panicking because kissing Reid was a point of no return.

Maybe I wasn't prepared to be gravely disappointed in the kiss? Maybe I wasn't ready to be over my crush yet. Yep, that's why I'd run. Because I wasn't prepared to be disappointed. Wasn't ready to let go of my infatuation yet. Perhaps after the wedding?

But if I'd only been trying to avoid the potential of disappointment, then why was I shaking? Why was I running away?

Because the truth wasn't that I was avoiding a disappointment in our kiss. The real fear was if he'd been good at it.

Chapter Thirteen
REID

"What the hell just happened?" I asked an empty room. I'd never seen Teagan react the way she had. So frazzled and, well, awkward. Had she freaked out about the impending kiss?

I blew air into my hand to double-check it hadn't been my breath. Was she having second thoughts about doing this fake relationship? I knew I was. Almost daily. Not because I didn't look forward to bringing her to the wedding but because of how my body had been reacting to hers.

Grab her ass.

I shook my head at her ridiculous request. Clearly, she'd been joking with me, but I wasn't willing to cross that line. I wasn't blind. Her ass was in fact spectacular, but appreciation and taking action were two different things.

It had been her idea to initiate the kiss, but maybe the thought of actually doing so with her boss had freaked her out at the last minute. Not for the first time, I wondered if putting her in this position was healthy for our work relationship.

Mulling it over, I became determined to let her off the hook. Attending the wedding solo would be difficult and somewhat painful, but it was only going to be a few days, and I was a grown man. I could handle seeing my ex and not let the pain over her betrayal dictate my self-esteem.

The next morning, I sent Teagan a text to cancel our gym meet. If I was calling this off, I'd do it in the office. Hell, that's where this whole fake girlfriend idea had been born, so it was only fitting to end it in the same place. And something about donning a suit and tie made me feel more in control of this personal connection we'd been forming. It was one thing to become friendly with Teagan but quite another to fake kissing.

As soon as I saw the notification she'd logged in to her computer, I sent her a message to come into my office. The first thing I noticed was that she appeared tired. Maybe she truly had needed to go to a "thing" last night, and whatever it was had kept her out late. An expected tinge of jealousy hit me. I didn't know what she did with her evenings or who she did it with. Did this have anything to do with the mark on her face? I had to remind myself it wasn't any of my business. Especially if I was ending our agreement.

"Hi," I started out, experiencing unexpected nerves.

"Hi. Sorry I'm late this morning."

My lips tipped up. "You're not late. I'm early for a change. How was your thing last night?"

"What thing?" she questioned before seemingly catching herself. "Oh, yeah, it was just a thing I had to do. I'd forgotten about it."

I knew it. She'd been lying. "Mm, does this thing have a name?"

"Um, I was supposed to FaceTime my sister and niece and we set these times to eat dinner together—I mean dinner for me, breakfast for them because of the time difference, you know—so I had to go."

"Ah." Teagan was a terrible liar. She was rambling and wouldn't meet my gaze. "I've been doing a lot of thinking lately."

Now her beautiful green eyes did focus on me.

"I don't know if it's a good idea, after all, for you to go to the wedding and pretend to be my girlfriend. Please know I appreciate the offer, but I realized it's asking too much."

She arched a brow. "Are you fake breaking up with me?"

"It's clear you weren't comfortable last night. Asking you to kiss your boss is way too much."

"It's not too much. Here, let's do it and just get it over with." She moved closer to me.

"Here in the office?" My voice went up an octave.

"Why not? Not like I'm getting naked on your desk. Now kiss me, unless you're the one freaking out about it?"

Chapter Fourteen
TEAGAN

I was a liar, liar, pants on fire. I had freaked out. But now I was freaking out even more in fear my freak-out may have jeopardized the entire thing. I'd never get over my crush if I didn't take this opportunity now. Not to mention I'd have to give up spending time with Reid. At this point, that sounded like a very lonely option.

Misdirection. It was the cornerstone of my survival. Therefore, I was turning his concern back on him.

"If you've changed your mind about wanting me to go with you because it's too uncomfortable for you, then I guess I understand." There was a good chance that after hanging out with me every day and learning about my background, he'd reversed his thinking about introducing me to his family. I didn't exactly come with the upbringing his wealthy family would expect. And although I'd mastered faking it over the years, this wedding would be a whole other league.

"No. But I don't want it to be weird between us. Not just because I'm your boss, since we're only in Dubai together for a short time longer, but because we're friends too."

This was the fundamental sweetness and flaw of Reid. He

always put others first. And I'd bet his fiancée had used this to her advantage many times.

"I promise it won't get weird. It's natural to be awkward at first, but like you said, we're friends. It'll be fine."

Okay. I could do this. It would be a simple kiss, not a life-changing orgasm. Dammit, don't think about orgasms.

"If it's too awkward, or you've changed your mind, my offer stands. We can opt out."

"No. No. It's not too awkward. Pfft." Jesus, this pfft thing was getting out of control.

He smirked, stepping closer to me. "You certain you don't have anywhere else you have to be? No forgotten appointments this time around?"

Oh, damn, his voice did this husky thing, making my tummy flop.

"Nope, no appointments." My pulse leaped the moment his fingers touched my chin. Guess it was a better reaction than throwing up.

"Good."

Please, please let this suck.

The moment his lips met mine, I knew my wish would go ungranted. With no more than the chaste brush of his lips, I was fucked. And not in a good way.

He pulled back after the brief touch. "So far so good?"

"Mm-hm." My answer was as fried as my brain.

"Again?"

"Mm-hm." Apparently, I'd been reduced to a copy-and-paste answer.

He moved forward, touching his lips to mine again but this time not withdrawing. Instead, he pulled me closer and deepened the kiss. Suddenly, instead of standing there stunned, my body woke up to say, "hey, dumbass, how about you kiss him back?"

I tilted my head in order to allow him better access, barely stifling a moan when his tongue met mine. Just my luck. Reid was a terrific kisser. I wasn't sure my heart could take it. My body, on the other hand, was ready for more.

But abruptly, he stepped away. "Um. So, yeah. There's kissing."

"Mm-hm." *Dammit, vocabulary, get it together.*

His blue eyes trained on mine. "Was it okay?"

Nope. Not at all. I was in serious trouble.

But I vowed not to answer another question with "mm-hm." "Um, yeah." Jesus. I'd been rendered completely ridiculous. My brain stammered back on track. "I mean yes. I think we'll be convincing."

My crush had decided to amplify to twenty times its previous size, entering a place we'd label the danger zone. The area where I could no longer contain my feelings, and I ended up getting my heart broken.

He expelled a breath, appearing relieved the kiss hadn't sent me running. Who could blame him, considering the way I'd bolted the last time.

But other than relief, he seemed absolutely unaffected by the kiss. It had been practice for him. Going through the motions. It had been earth-shattering for me. Okay, so maybe earth-shattering was an exaggeration, but it had been a really great kiss. One which left me wanting more.

Irritation that I was the only one affected fueled my motivation to change the subject. "Um, so what's on the agenda for this week?"

He stepped back, moving to take a seat at his desk. "You need to go shopping for clothes."

Sigh. I was not a shopping kind of girl. "Sounds great."

He chuckled. "Great is not what your face is saying."

Busted. "I'm not much on shopping, especially for

clothes." Growing up poor, I'd mostly relied on hand-me-downs. Shopping was always a depressing endeavor where all I saw were things I couldn't afford.

"I don't think I've ever heard a woman say she didn't enjoy shopping."

"It'll be fine. Just tell me what I'll need. I already have a cocktail dress and a long floral dress." I didn't have a lot of coin to be spending on new clothes, but I could find some stuff on sale and make it work.

His hesitation wasn't lost on me.

"What?"

"This crowd. My family. They'll be paying attention to which designers you're wearing. Especially Vanessa. She's into fashion and up on all of the trends."

My clothing wouldn't cut it, I supposed. I tried not to let it sting or allow my old insecurity about not feeling good enough rear its ugly head. "Makes sense."

"How about we go tonight after work?"

"You're coming with me?"

"Yes. Of course. I'm paying."

I didn't like the idea of him paying for my clothes. But I definitely didn't have the money for designer threads either. "Okay. Tonight it is."

Chapter Fifteen

REID

I pushed all thoughts of our kiss aside until she left my office. Damn. I was in trouble.

It was one thing to figure it was inevitable for any man, including me, to experience an attraction to a beautiful woman like Teagan. But it was quite another to realize my attraction had shifted to craving. I wanted another taste of her. Our kiss was in my head on constant repeat. The way her lips had been soft. The way she'd been unexpectedly shy at first but then had seemed to awaken. Or the way her breath had caught, and she'd seemed to sink into it when my tongue had tangled with hers.

Jesus, my imagination was running overtime. Just because I was having this reaction to our kiss didn't mean it was reciprocated. If Teagan Larson was interested in a man, I had no doubt she would not be shy about telling him.

The prospect of more "fake kisses" was beginning to mess with my head. What would happen if she realized I was no longer faking it?

That night after work, we headed to the Mall of the Emirates. Dubai might be the desert and a conservative nation, but the malls were a sight to see. Hell, this one was six million, five hundred thousand square feet and boasted an indoor skiing facility.

I already knew Teagan was unlike other women I'd known, but I didn't realize how different she truly was until we parked in the giant lot. Vanessa would've been giddy with excitement at the prospect of shopping. Teagan, on the other hand, seemed as though she was heading for an execution.

If her lack of enthusiasm meant we could get in and out quickly, then perhaps it wasn't such a bad thing. I wasn't exactly big on shopping either.

"I figure we'll hit the Harvey Nichols department store first, and see what they have. You okay with that plan?"

She simply nodded. She'd been uncharacteristically quiet ever since we'd left the office.

"Everything okay?" I was concerned she might be feeling weird after our kiss earlier. Worse, she might have realized how hard it had been for me to pull away.

"I'd tell you if it wasn't."

Of course she would. I needed to stop imagining she was uncomfortable and instead worry about how I could keep my attraction in check. "Okay, let's go shopping."

We headed into the department store. Today, Teagan had worn a green wrap dress to the office. Now that I was thinking more about her, I noticed how the color brought out her eyes while the cut of the dress set off her curves.

"What sort of things do I need?" she asked.

"It's a beach wedding, but the ceremony is to be quite formal, so you'll need a mix of beach casual to dressy. I made a list."

She made a face when I presented it to her. "That's a long list. When does the mall close?"

She was right. It was a long list. There would be a cocktail reception, the rehearsal dinner, and, of course, the wedding. "The mall doesn't close until nine o'clock, which gives us about three hours. What we don't get tonight, we can get tomorrow."

Her sigh made me smile.

"Why don't we start with a dress for the wedding itself?"

Over the next ten minutes, I learned a few things about Teagan. She avoided anything red, pink, coral, or orange, she bit on her thumb when she was anxious, and she seemed absolutely out of her element.

"What's wrong?" We'd been circling the same racks of dresses. Although I'd suggested a few, she hadn't selected anything to try on.

She gave me a look but wouldn't reply.

"Teagan, tell me."

Finally she turned to face me and whispered even though we were alone. "These clothes are thousands of dollars. You cannot expect me to wear anything that costs more than a rent payment."

Ah. When was the last time I'd been with a woman who cared what I was about to spend on her? The answer was never. "I wouldn't have suggested you pick whatever you wanted if I was worried about the expense. Consider them gifts for doing me such a big favor. Now, how about you don't even peek at the price tags?"

She huffed, rolled her neck, and blew out a long breath. "Fine."

"And if you're not fond of what you find here, we can go to other stores."

"Shoot me now. No. This store should do fine. But afterwards we're eating a carb-filled dinner to make up for this torture."

My laughter came easily. I found myself amused at the

way she was so prickly about shopping. "Absolutely. Lady's choice for dinner."

Thirty minutes later, we were done with dresses—she'd selected four—and moved on to the shoe department. I watched her take stock, looking like she was at a meat counter perusing the ground beef choices instead of picking out shoes. Every woman I knew had a weakness for shoes, but once again, Teagan was proving me wrong.

"The sandals there should do." She pointed at a black strappy sandal, and the salesman quickly departed to fetch her size. "It'll go with all of the outfits."

"You need to find at least four more pair. Casual for the days, and dressed up for the nights."

"But the black goes with everything."

"Yes, but you can't go wearing the same pair of shoes with each outfit. People would notice." I was trying to save her from any judgment by the other guests. Teagan might have grown up poor, but I didn't want her to feel lacking in anything at this wedding. I wanted her to feel like she belonged.

"We wouldn't want that. Okay, fine, I'll pick some more."

We were in and out of the shoe department in record time with a less-than-happy Teagan holding her purchases. I suspected the next chore would probably send her through the roof.

"You'll need a bikini or two. And other beach stuff."

Her glare would've slayed a lesser man.

I was not a lesser man. And frankly, the prospect of seeing Teagan in a bikini wasn't such a hardship. "It's a beach wedding, which means there will be a beach."

She rolled her eyes. "Designer beachwear? There's such a thing?"

"Indeed. And it'll include new sunglasses, a hat, and a

cover-up. Then we'll go over to the purses. You'll need one for day and a couple for night."

Her narrowed gaze made me grin.

"Come on, it won't be that bad."

"Lead on, but know I'm getting my revenge tomorrow night after work."

"At the gym?"

She smirked. "You will only wish it was the gym."

Chapter Sixteen
TEAGAN

I plotted my revenge while trying on swimsuits in the ladies' lounge. Reid didn't know it yet, but he was soon to become my beauty treatment guinea pig. Not that getting a facial was high on the torture spectrum, but for a man like Reid, I imagined it would be an uncomfortable, somewhat embarrassing thing to endure. I sighed, wanting to be more grateful, especially since he was dropping thousands on my new wardrobe. But I couldn't muster gratitude. The price tags made me sick to my stomach. Honestly, though, it wasn't merely the cost that bothered me. What truly upset me was the realization that my Old Navy meets H&M wardrobe would never be good enough for Reid or his family. The thought weighed heavily, but I had to keep things in perspective. I was his fake girlfriend, and regardless of my feelings for him and the fact our first kiss had rocked my world, I couldn't ever be anything more.

An hour later I was finally done with the tortuous enterprise. "I have no idea how I'll fit all of these clothes into my suitcase," I grumbled as we walked out to the car, both of us laden with bags.

He snapped his fingers. "I almost forgot. We need to get you some new luggage."

I practically hissed at the suggestion. I was hungry, I was grumpy, and I was done.

He chuckled, dropping his stuff in the back of his Land Rover before holding up both hands in surrender. "Relax. I'll pick something up for you."

"Fine." I gritted the words out and got into the passenger side of his vehicle like a petulant child. One who needed chili cheese fries stat.

"What's your dining pleasure?"

"Fran's Diner off of Main and Seventh."

He glanced over, his lips twitching. "You got it."

We didn't speak again until we were seated in the retro booth, outfitted with everything down to a mini jukebox on the table. I loved this restaurant and all of the American diner nostalgia.

"How did you find this place?" he asked.

"Chloe and I have been here a few times. It's American comfort food at its finest."

"Does that mean you won't judge when I get the pot roast and mashed potatoes?"

I shook my head. "Nope, just like you won't judge when I eat an entire platter of chili cheese fries."

He studied me. "Tonight's expedition was chili-cheese-fries bad, huh?"

I closed my menu. "Chili-cheese-fries-and-a-chocolate-milkshake bad."

When the waitress came over, we both rattled off our orders and sat back in our seats to relax. I didn't like the way he was studying me. It was as if he could read why I'd been so uncomfortable in the fancy department stores.

"I'm sorry you didn't enjoy shopping."

Guilt crept up. He'd spent a lot of money, and here I was acting ungrateful. "I'm sorry for being a brat. I appreciate the clothes, I honestly do. But accepting that much money being spent on me is difficult."

"Why?"

Such a simple question but loaded with a lot more than I wished to discuss. "Well, we're not really dating, for one."

He cocked his head to the side. "And if we were, would you have felt more comfortable letting me buy you things?"

"No. If anything, I'd probably hate it more." At least in our present scenario, I could justify the expense because I was doing him a favor, and he was dressing me for the part.

"Why?"

Why did he push? "I don't know, okay."

He shook his head. "I don't believe you. But if you don't want to talk about it, just say so."

He was giving me an easy out. But I'd made him open up about less-than-pleasant topics like his ex. I also felt like I was acting chicken, unwilling to peel a layer back. "I'm not used to receiving gifts."

"You didn't get gifts growing up? Christmas? Birthdays?"

Tears threatened to spring to my eyes at the way he asked. Not with judgment, but with genuine kindness. I chose to shake my head instead of verbally responding.

He muttered a curse under his breath, so I had to speak up to amend his perception. "My sister would try. She'd make something or find something. I tried to do the same for her once I was old enough to be creative. After she adopted me when I was fourteen, we had our first Christmas together in this shitty apartment with a sad tree and a single string of lights. We gave each other gifts from the dollar store, and spent the day at the beach. Neither of us had ever been happier."

He swallowed hard. "How bad was the time in foster care?"

I didn't talk about it. Ever. Not even to my sister. Especially not to my sister. She'd get this guilty look in her eyes as if it was her fault she hadn't been able to adopt me until she'd turned eighteen. But Reid was my friend, and considering how much he'd shared with me, it seemed only fair to give him something.

"My foster parents were nice people and lived in a good neighborhood. But being a foster kid in an affluent neighborhood was its own personal hell. Anyhow, as far as foster situations go, mine wasn't horrible."

So what if I got punched in the stomach daily by another seventeen-year-old foster kid because, in her words, "your breathing bothers me"? So what if I had to wake up at three o'clock in the morning to take a shower before the two teenage boys were up because otherwise they'd leer and try to cop a feel? So what if the girls at school would make fun of my ill-fitting clothes, and the boys would taunt me mercilessly for not having parents who wanted me. At least it had only been for a few months.

"You're leaving a lot out, aren't you?"

I was saved from having to provide an answer when the waitress returned with our food.

Two minutes into my meal, Reid was watching me. "You realize stuffing your face with chili cheese fries doesn't make the question go away."

I turned to my milkshake next. "I disagree. And this is off-limits for a fake relationship."

"There is nothing fake about our friendship. But if you don't want to talk about it, like I said before, I understand." He paused, taking a bite of pot roast and making a sound of pleasure which put my entire body on notice.

Right. Friendship. Down, girl. "It's not easy for me to talk about. My sister doesn't even know all the details. If I could block the memories, I would. From the stories I've heard about foster care, it could've been much worse."

"It can always be worse. The problems others suffer can put things in perspective, but that doesn't mean what you went through was easy."

Chapter Seventeen
REID

I studied Teagan from across the table, seeing the vulnerability in her eyes. As I heard about her time in foster care, I had no doubt she was omitting a great deal. As much as I respected her privacy, I found myself wishing she'd share more. Hell, at this point, I wanted nothing more than to jump on the other side of the booth and comfort her with a hug. I doubted she'd appreciate the gesture, though, as it wouldn't fit in with her tough-girl image.

She ate her fries but then sighed, giving me more clues about her childhood. "I didn't always have thick skin and a sharp tongue."

"I would dare to say no one starts out life with either of those attributes. They're normally hard earned."

She only played with her straw, declining to elaborate on my opening. Despite my craving for more information, perhaps it was time for a break from the serious stuff.

"So tell me, are you the type of girlfriend who shares her fries?"

The shadows left her eyes, and a smile replaced the tension. "What do you think?"

"I think I could lose a hand if I reached over to help myself."

"Smart man. But I'm not opposed to a trade. Say, for a bite of your pot roast with potatoes?"

I forked up a perfectly proportioned bite, including the gravy, and held it across the table toward her amused face. But once her lips closed around my fork, my grin dropped. How could offering her a bite of pot roast make my dick hard?

Jesus, ever since our kiss, I'd become hyper-focused on every detail about her. At this point, if she moaned, I could go on to embarrass myself. Luckily for me, she only smiled.

"Damn, you made this trade well worth it. All right, you earned it." She lifted up a section of her chili cheese fries on a fork before passing it to me.

The flavors were incredible. "I can see now why you wouldn't want to share."

"Exactly. Now then, spill it. How was your childhood?"

In contrast, my childhood had been privileged, rich, and indulgent—although not without its problems. "My dad and mom divorced when I was ten, so I spent a lot of time with Aiden's family and with Mona, the live-in nanny." I was closer to her while growing up than to either of my parents. Although she'd retired to Arizona, I still kept in touch with her. "My dad has been married three more times since my mother, each new bride younger than the last. His current wife is my age, and I'm assuming may be pregnant soon since he's had kids with each of his wives. All of the kids are boys except for one."

Teagan let out a low whistle. "Must make for an interesting family tree."

"That's an understatement."

"Are you close with any of your siblings?"

Chance and I used to be tight. "I'm close with my half sister, Kelsey, who's about your age. But the rest of my brothers, not so much. In my defense, though, the twins are five years old."

She about spit out her drink. "That would be so weird. You could basically be their dad."

"At this rate and given the trajectory of his brides, I will probably be old enough to be his next wife's father."

This time her drink caught in her throat, and she started coughing. I moved over to her side of the booth to thump her back. It wasn't a hardship to have an excuse to sit close to her.

"Thanks for the assist. I can't imagine that image. Will any of your family be at the wedding?"

Now that she could breathe again, I had no choice but to return to my side of the table. "My mother will be there. But my father wouldn't want to leave his business. Not sure about Chance." He knew the groom too, but I doubted he'd bother to come to a destination wedding.

"What's your dad's business?"

"He owns a private investment company. He invests in dozens of other companies and sits on the board for several." He was a billionaire who valued his company above any human interaction.

"Did he want you to follow in his footsteps?"

"He did, but Chance and I preferred to make our own way."

"You didn't like the business, or you didn't like working for your dad?"

"Both. My father enjoys having control, and how better than to have your children working for you? I couldn't do it.

Not for him nor for Vanessa's father who wanted me to work at his tech company." It was a source of pride for me to have broken away and become successful without my father's influence or money. "My dad was annoyed at first, but he's come around." He was reluctantly proud.

"Are you close with your mom?"

"I love my mother, but it's impossible to be close to her without some measure of drama, which means I often need a break. She's also bitter about the divorce. She hasn't forgiven my father for having an affair despite having had several of her own. The only difference was my father left her for his."

"Yikes. You mentioned people wanting you and your ex to get back together. Does that include your mom?"

"It does. My mother and Vanessa's mother have wanted us to marry for years. They're friends, and I think it's a source of pride for her to have our two families merge."

"Sounds like another world."

"It is." One I was happy to no longer be a part of. Thinking about it now, I realized something strange. I'd been anxious to break away from the bubble of privilege I'd grown up in, but as long as I'd stayed with Vanessa, that meant I never truly could.

"So I believe I have the lay of the land on your ex and now your family. What about the groom and your friends who will be there?"

"The groom, Kevin, is someone I grew up with. He's marrying Vanessa's cousin. And I went to undergrad with some of the other groomsmen. Phil will be there. He and his wife, Ellen, are normal people. Word of warning: she may be the solitary woman there who will be nice to you."

Teagan lifted a shoulder. "Don't worry."

Right. I'd try not to.

"Stay right here, and close your eyes. Hold still."

The following evening we were at my apartment. Teagan's idea of retribution for the shopping trip was to give me a facial. She assumed I'd find the idea of pampering absolute torture, but it wasn't the cool mask on my face responsible for making me uncomfortable. Nope, it was the touch of her fingers over my skin, the nearness of her so I could pick up her signature scent of coconut, and the way my body was reacting to her.

"What are you going to do to me?" Damn, my voice was much huskier than I'd intended. But in my defense, she was leaning right over my position where I lay on the sofa with my head propped on the arm of it.

"That first step was cleansing your face." Although my eyes were closed, I could hear the smirk in her voice. Quick little dabs with her cotton rounds were efficiently gliding along my skin. Next came something cold. "The substance I'm applying now is a mask."

Once she was done spreading the goop on my face, she started massaging my hand.

I couldn't help tensing up.

"Sorry, part of giving a facial is typically a little massage of the arms and hands, but if you don't want me to—"

"No, no, it's fine." Pathetically, I could feel my cock already liking the idea. *Jesus, get it together.*

"The mask will make your skin brighter."

"Are you saying my skin is dull?" I was kidding, yet her response hit me directly in the solar plexus.

"There's nothing dull about you, Reid Maxwell."

Bitterness laced my response. "My ex would disagree with you. I tend to be a creature of habit." She'd always admonished me about how I'd order the same meal in a restaurant, wore the same brand of shirt in different colors, and had worn the same style haircut since college.

"Your ex is a cunt."

I tried to smile, but my face was covered in a creamy substance smelling of marshmallows. Teagan's bluntness cracked me up. "And now I know you don't flinch at using the C-word."

"Not for a woman who cheated on her fiancé with his older brother during a family holiday party. Yeah, she's the definition of the word. But not to worry, I won't go dropping C-bombs at the wedding. Oh, unless you give me whiskey. Whiskey makes me feisty."

My chuckle filled the room. "You mean there's such a thing as another level up?"

"What are you implying? You think I'm feisty now? Let me guess: it's my red hair."

"Your red hair has nothing to do with what makes you feisty. And it was meant to be a compliment."

"Is it? It seems most men don't want a woman who speaks her mind, says the C-word from time to time, or doesn't take shit from people."

I contemplated the vulnerability edging her words. "Then I'd argue you haven't found the right man yet." I paused, wondering who could be the right man for Teagan. "What, uh, would you look for in a potential mate?"

She gave a snort of laughter. "Please don't say mate ever again. Makes me feel like a goat."

My smile was tough to manage with the goo tightening my face. At least I was now able to open my eyes. "Why would you say a goat, of all animals?"

She shrugged while I bit back a groan of pleasure at the

way she was now massaging my hands. "Goats mate same as any other animal, I suppose."

I needed to get off of the mating topic. "True. By the way, how exactly is this payback for our shopping trip?" I thoroughly enjoyed the way her strong hands kneaded my arm, and tried not to notice how she was now leaning over me, the soft swell of her breasts inches from my face.

"I may have underestimated how much you'd enjoy being my guinea pig."

"So tell me again. You finished cosmetology school?"

"No, not quite. I had a few more classes to go."

I focused on her face. Her expression showed concentration as she massaged my left hand. Never would I have thought a hand massage would feel so good. "You miss it?"

"Mm, sometimes. But it's probably better as a hobby. Friends-and-family type of thing."

"Why? You could go work at a spa."

Her eyes locked with mine, and I knew in an instant I'd asked the wrong question.

"It probably doesn't pay as much as the assistant position, I take it?" I inquired quietly.

"No, it doesn't. Anyhow, your mask is set, so I'll grab some warm water and get it off of you."

I opened my jaw, feeling the mask crackle as a result. "'Kay, what's next?"

"Let's order some food."

Chapter Eighteen
TEAGAN

I needed a moment to step away from Reid. He was too adorable, lying on his couch and being such a great sport. Giving him a facial was bliss for me, and something I could see doing for my boyfriend after work. What it wasn't however was getting me out of the danger zone. I could easily and completely fall for him.

So much for torturing him. I was the one tortured by the necessity of touching him during the whole process. Jesus, even his pores were perfect. So unfair. I busied myself in his kitchen, washing out the towels in the sink and grabbing a warm bowl of water.

"How about instead of ordering in tonight, we go out? There's a restaurant across the street from the office that's good," Reid suggested while I removed his mask.

Chloe had told me about the place. It was a fancy steakhouse she'd gone to with Aiden. It had linen tablecloths, a fancy menu, an even fancier wine list, and way too many forks in my opinion. Which brought about another area of anxiety. Table manners had never been a high priority when you were lucky to have even one meal a day—often subsidized by the school. Sure, I knew to eat with my mouth closed and keep my elbows off the table, but that was the extent of my knowledge of etiquette.

"I'd prefer to eat in, if you don't mind." After removing his mask, I put a layer of moisturizer over his skin and marveled at how soft it was.

After cleaning up and using the restroom, I walked back out to the living room to see him inspecting his face in the mirror. The way he kept touching his newly exfoliated skin made me smile.

His gaze landed on me. "I don't mind eating in."

Relief flowed through me. I needed to do some research on table etiquette. Yep, I needed to buy some time and learn some things before I left for the wedding. Two days. I could do it. Watch some YouTube videos. Call Chloe. She'd know what to do.

For tonight, I sat on Reid's couch, eating Chinese food off his coffee table and dressed in leggings and a baggy T-shirt that said, "Some days it's not worth chewing through the restraints." Once we'd eaten and I had a game controller in my hand, I finally felt less anxious. But I also felt bad. He probably missed going to restaurants and hadn't wanted to go alone.

Reid got his game console ready to play.

"I'm sorry we didn't go out," I told him. "You could say I'm a homebody."

"Hey, I am too. Guess I needed to ensure I wasn't forcing my homebody, boring self on you."

"That's the second time you've mentioned being dull or boring."

"Yes, and the polite thing to do would be to ignore it and pretend I wasn't voicing an insecurity." With the remote, he brought up Mario Kart Racing. It was by far my favorite game, and I was still touched he'd bought a new gaming system just so we could play it.

"Mm, ignoring something isn't really my style. Did the twat of the ex give you a complex about being boring?"

He sighed, probably not happy I wasn't letting this go.

I picked my character, ready to race.

"She was into the night life, you know, parties and clubs, and I wasn't. She said my inability to try new things was one of the reasons we didn't work."

I snorted with laughter. "I'd say your brother's penis in her mouth would be the major reason it didn't work, but hey, who am I to judge?"

His cringe made me immediately regret my unfiltered words.

"Sorry. My joke is funnier if you're not the one who she cheated on."

"No, no," he was quick to reassure me. "It was funny. I was just thinking...it's Chance's birthday tomorrow."

Ah, the asshole brother. "I take it you won't call him."

"No, I won't. It'll be the first time I don't wish him a happy birthday."

I couldn't imagine being on the outs with my sister to the point I couldn't talk to her. Then again, I couldn't imagine the pain if she'd cheated with my fiancé either. "Did he ever apologize? You mentioned your ex blew up your phone with saying she was sorry, but has he?"

"Apologies aren't Chance's style. He probably believes I should be thanking him for keeping me from marrying someone who would cheat."

"Talk about twisting things." Yet in a weird way, Chance actually had saved Reid from spending a lifetime with a cheater. Some people would say they'd take a bullet for a sibling; perhaps Chance had decided to take a blowjob for his brother?

Reid sighed. "How did we end up on this subject again? You must be completely sick of talking about my ex or anything having to do with it."

"It's healthy to talk about it instead of bottling it all up and pretending you've erased it from your mind." That's what my sister had done when her boyfriend had up and left her with a newborn. She erased him from her life and refused to acknowledge his existence, not even going after him for much-needed child support.

"I don't know. Erasing it sounds pretty good. Guess it's a good thing again we're not actually dating. Otherwise, I'd say I'm failing spectacularly. Yet another reminder to wait before getting back out there."

Made sense. He should wait. It was clear he wasn't anywhere close to being over his ex and what had happened. "Hey, as your friend, I should remind you we need to hit the gym hard tomorrow to make up for this salty Chinese food. You've cancelled the last two mornings."

"I'm already down eight pounds, I'll have you know."

"It's so unfair for men to be able to drop weight so quickly."

"I know. But regardless of whether it's fair or not, I'll take my loss as a victory. To the gym it is. We only have two days until we leave. Oh, which reminds me. I bought you luggage."

He got up and went into his bedroom, returning with two pieces of brown leather luggage.

"No way."

"What?" He appeared confused by my expression of horror.

"That's Louis Vuitton luggage." I didn't know a lot of designers, but I knew Louis.

"Yep, it sure is."

"This is too much. Is someone seriously going to judge my luggage and say, 'OMG, does she have Samsonite luggage? What a loser'?" Suddenly I was in jeopardy of puking up my Chinese food.

He chuckled. "Believe me, they'll be dissecting every detail. And for the record, there is nothing wrong with Samsonite luggage. It's what I have."

"Then why the hell would you get me this fancy stuff? You have to return it."

"You're being serious?"

"Yes. How can you possibly justify spending that kind of money on luggage? By the way, it goes under the plane and gets dirty, beat up, and often lost. Fancy luggage like that is a flashing neon sign telling people to steal it."

He seemed to contemplate. "Good point. I'll return it tomorrow and get you something else."

"Samsonite. Black. Or blue if you're feeling fancy. But plain luggage, Reid. I mean it."

"Yes, ma'am. Now will you calm down and stop looking like you're tempted to chuck your controller at my head? We wouldn't want to scar this handsome face right before the big weekend, now, would we?"

I realized I was indeed gripping the device as though I was ready to throw a major tantrum and take out an innocent controller in the process. "Standing down now." I cracked a smile and sat back down on the couch.

"Phew, that was intense." He took a seat beside me. "You were really angry."

"Damn right I was. Designer luggage is a ridiculous expense." On the other hand, if I was searching for a turnoff, the way he was so careless with his money could be it. But the problem was he wasn't spending it on himself. He was being generous. Which wasn't a turnoff. Dammit.

"I guess when you put it the way you did, it is rather silly to have expensive luggage. Now then, you ready to lose the next game?"

"Ha. I'll have you know I'm an excellent driver."

I wasn't, but it didn't matter. I had the best time regardless of my inability to come in any higher than sixth place.

"Hey, Teagan, you sounded stressed, what's the emergency?"

Chloe's face came into view over my FaceTime screen, making me miss her fiercely. I was in serious need of my best friend and her advice as I sat on my sofa at six o'clock in the morning my time. I only had one more day in the office before my trip. "The emergency is manners. I need some. Stat."

She giggled. "Um, I'll overnight them via FedEx? What's going on?"

Where to start? "Well, I'm flying out early tomorrow morning for the Turks and Caicos to attend a wedding with Reid as his fake girlfriend. There will be fancy dinners and the reception, and I'm panicked. I'm not equipped to be around rich people with all those forks and knives on the table."

I had to give her credit for taking the news in stride. She did a slow blink with wide eyes. "I know it's early there, and you need to get ready for work soon, but I need a summarized version of how all of that came to be."

"Long story short, I finally had my little intervention about Reid's moping. He has this wedding where he'll have to see his ex—it was originally to be in Boston but got moved to the islands and is this weekend. When I suggested he take a date, he asked me if I'd go. To act as his fake girlfriend."

A smile spread across Chloe's beautiful face. "And how is faking it with your crush?"

"Oh, you know. Torture, and a tale for when I have more time. Can you help me, Chloe Bear?"

She let out a long sigh. "I'm not exactly the type to win any Miss Manners contests, but I'll try. Hold up. Let me get Kendall. She's been to more fancy dinners than I have. If you're okay with it?"

Kendall was Chloe's previous roommate and was married to Liam, who'd been Kendall's boss. I could bet she'd been to a fancy dinner a time or two. "Of course. I'll take any advice I can get."

A minute later, a beautiful brunette came into view. "Hi, Teagan, I've heard so much about you. Okay. So Chloe says you need help with table manners."

"Desperately."

"Okay. Let's see. When you first sit down, put the napkin in your lap. Your drink is on your right, but sometimes I forget and wait until my neighbor picks up their drink."

"What about the forks?" I had viewed a YouTube video, but it had been overwhelming.

"Start on the outside and work your way in."

"Okay." I was stressed.

"Don't be too anxious, Teag. Just do the normal by sitting up straight, no elbows on the table, and chew with your mouth closed."

"What if I have to use the restroom? What happens to the napkin?"

"Put it on your chair?" Kendall threw a questioning look toward Chloe as she answered.

Shrugging, Chloe brought out her phone to search for the answer. "Yep, Google says it goes on the chair. So it must be true. Oh, rip your bread or roll into pieces and don't bite into it."

It was some shit when a roll had proper etiquette.

"Honestly, I just mimic what other people do," Chloe offered.

That's what I'd have to do too. "Thank you both. My initial panic has eased. I'll watch some more YouTube before we leave."

"Have you fake kissed him yet?" Chloe asked.

My entire face heated. "Yeah. Once."

"And?"

"And it was amazing for me and awkward for him."

Her lips flattened. "Maybe it was awkward because he felt something?"

Leave it to Chloe to look on the bright side. "I appreciate the optimism, but I'm the Cheez Whiz to his brie."

"That's absurd. Don't you dare insult yourself that way. I don't know Reid like you do, but I'm convinced he's not the type to stand on pretense or believe he's better for having money."

Maybe. But the designer clothes and my need to make up a fictitious background made it clear I wasn't real girlfriend material. But I'd put on the act for him. I'd pretend to be better than my upbringing. "Doesn't matter. He applied for a job in Australia, and I'll probably move to LA in a few months."

Chloe sighed. "Selfishly, I'll be happy to have you here in LA. Maybe we could become roommates again."

I kept my mouth shut, but I was thinking that if Aiden followed through with his plans, she most likely would be living with him. But I couldn't give her any clues because there was always the chance he could mess it up. Let's hope not as she deserved a happy ending.

As much as I hoped the words would come true for her, I wasn't sure I believed in a happy ending. The whole concept seemed more fiction than real world. Like the family with a mother and father I used to dream about, who ate dinner together, genuinely loved and supported each other.

I wasn't sure that sort of thing was in the cards for me. I supposed if I were to define the perfect man, it would be someone who got me. Who wasn't intimidated by my personality and maybe thought my sarcasm and armor weren't off-putting.

"In all the chaos, I almost forgot to mention I'm heading to LA after this trip. I'll be there Monday."

Chloe squealed. "Best news ever. I can't wait to hear all about your weekend. Have fun and call me once you land. Okay?"

"Definitely."

In the meantime, since getting over my crush hadn't worked thus far, I was settling for a new plan of avoiding a broken heart.

Chapter Nineteen

REID

Teagan and I had been so busy the last few days that I hadn't had time to worry about how everyone at the wedding would react to me bringing a date. Until now. At two am in the Emirates check-in line at the Dubai airport.

"You okay?" she asked.

She appeared cool as a cucumber and looked adorable, wearing flip-flops, black sweatpants, and an oversized T-shirt with the words, "Not a hugger" under a picture of a cactus. She'd straightened her hair, which was a much different look for her.

"If you're worried about what I'm wearing, I brought clothes to change into on the plane."

"No, no, it's a long flight. You should be comfortable. I'm fine. Are you okay?" She'd been quiet since I'd picked her up at her apartment. Then again, it was in the middle of the night —the downside of flying out of Dubai were the early morning flights.

"Yes. I'm good."

"You straightened your hair. Looks longer." It was nice,

but I had to admit I preferred her wilder curls. They seemed to match her personality better.

"I needed the hair to go with the designer clothes."

I hope she hadn't thought she had to go to the trouble. I'd wanted her to feel comfortable over the weekend, and able to withstand the judgy crowd, but I had to admit the result was making me uneasy. "Is this crazy? The entire thing?"

She lifted a perfectly arched brow before narrowing her eyes. "Nope. No way. Do not go getting cold feet now, Reid Maxwell. Not after I spent hours trying on clothes, straightening my hair, and I even studied etiquette, so I don't go getting the damn salad fork mixed up with the dinner fork."

I was shocked to hear she'd gone to such lengths. "You studied dining etiquette?"

She sighed, appearing uncharacteristically uneasy. "I would say it was more of a crash course to keep me from embarrassing you at one of the fancy dinners. Anyhow, we're up."

We were called up to the check-in desk, delaying our conversation. The gate agent checked our passports, took our luggage, and pointed us toward the Emirates business-class lounge. As we headed for the lounge, I found myself sincerely flattered at the effort Teagan had gone to so she'd fit in at the wedding, but at the same time, I didn't want her to think she had to change on my account.

"I hope you know you'd never embarrass me, Teagan."

She slid her gaze toward me. "Aw, you're so full of hope, I think you may actually believe that."

I couldn't help chuckling. Her humor was irresistible. "Seriously. I don't want you to feel uncomfortable."

"Oh, so I shouldn't feel uncomfortable in a crowd including your ex-fiancée, your brother who cheated with her, your mother you don't get along with, and a bunch of your country club friends who will probably watch my every move?"

I almost physically cringed. When she put it that way, I felt hard pressed to get on the flight. "Maybe we should head for Mexico instead."

"Ha, nice try."

We entered the opulent lounge and found seats at a table near the full-service bar. "Something to drink?"

"Mm. Ginger ale is good."

Yeah, alcohol at this hour didn't sound so appealing. So two ginger ales it was.

When I returned with her iced glass, she murmured a "thank you" before blowing out a long breath.

"You okay?"

"Yes. God, I hope we don't have to keep asking each other if we're okay this entire trip. Why are you so nervous?"

"Who said I was?"

She lifted that damn brow of hers again. "I recognize your signs. This relationship may be fake, but our friendship isn't."

My words thrown back at me. "Fine. I'm once again nervous about putting you in an awkward position. Maybe I should've gone solo. With my ex there and possibly my brother, there's no telling what kind of drama there may be."

She shrugged. "You may not get to choose what someone says, does, or acts, but you can control your reaction to it."

"Why do I get the impression you've learned that particular lesson the hard way?"

Her husky laugh hit me straight in the solar plexus. "It's an important lesson. The reaction is everything."

"Now why are you nervous?"

She hesitated. "I'm kind of an anxious flier."

"Seriously?" Her candor caught me off guard.

"Don't make a thing of it."

My laughter came easily but earned me a huff. "Come on," I said. "You being afraid of flying is a nice reminder you're human under all of your armor and sarcasm. Perhaps I need to discover more of your weaknesses."

"You mean my armor and sarcasm don't count as flaws?"

"Depends who you ask. Some people might find those attributes delightful." Like me, for instance. She was fun, smart, and all with an incredible sense of humor.

"Delightful is so not what I'm going for."

That much was obvious. Instead, it seemed she was hoping for unapproachable and unaffected. But over the last couple weeks, I'd learned those demeanors were her defense. Her mask to safeguard her vulnerable side.

"Where do you think you'll be in five years?" I found myself genuinely curious.

"Pass. Next question."

My lips twitched. "Come on. Humor me. We're killing time before the flight. Pick ten years if you want."

"I have no clue where I'll be in one year, let alone five or ten years."

"Okay, well, you don't plan on staying in Dubai, right?"

"No, I probably won't renew my contract again in three months."

"And you'll go back to LA, to be near your sister?"

"Most likely."

There seemed to be a quiet resignation to her response, as if it was something she felt compelled to do instead of something she wanted to do. "What would you do if there were no limits—if you could go anywhere or do anything?"

"Honestly?"

"Yes."

"I'd love to go live in another exotic city. I'd love to travel the world."

This didn't surprise me. Teagan had an energy that wouldn't want to be tied down or feel content with a place she'd already lived. "Delmont Security has offices all over the world." Such as in Sydney, where I'd applied. Wouldn't it be something if she chose to move there too? Was it wrong to hope she would?

"Yeah, but do you know what I really wish I could do?"

I leaned forward, feeling privileged she was about to share a secret. "What is it?"

"My dream job would be to go work in various spas in different amazing vacation spots around the world."

I could tell by the way she'd pampered me with the facial the other day that she'd enjoyed what she was doing. "What about having kids someday?" I was curious since I absolutely wanted children in my future.

"I love kids, but I see how hard my sister struggles with being a single mom—I just wouldn't want to go it alone. Which brings me back to relationships. I'm not certain I'm cut out for them."

"I could say the same given how I was in a long-term relationship that was completely dysfunctional. But I'd like to imagine there's someone else out there. Someone I'm meant to be with."

She bit her lip. "Do you ever think you missed your opportunity with Shelly, the girl you once dated while you and your ex had broken up? The one who developed feelings?"

The one I'd hurt by going back to Vanessa. "Nah, last I heard she was married and had a son. She deserved better than someone who was still in love with someone else. I hurt her, and I hate it."

"You need to stop beating yourself up about it. Sounds as if she moved on." Teagan was learning my cues.

"I know it." I did need to move on. But that didn't mean Shelly wouldn't serve as a lesson. A lesson to prevent me from ever acting on my attraction to Teagan. Even if she reciprocated the feeling, she deserved better than a man who was still grieving his last relationship. If I couldn't give my whole heart to someone new, then it was best I stay single for the time being.

Chapter Twenty
TEAGAN

It was clear Reid harbored some residual guilt over his relationship with Shelly and the fact he'd hurt her by going back to Vanessa. He was far from ready to move on from his latest breakup with her. Reason number—well, I lost track—that he was not the guy for me.

Ten years from now, he would probably have a house in an affluent suburb and a beautiful wife who volunteered at the private school where his two perfect kids attended. She'd have naturally straight hair, great table manners, and impeccable taste in designer clothes. He wouldn't have to worry about her dropping C-bombs or sharing depressing stories of her childhood. She'd eat brie, probably on a motherfucking carb-less cracker made of locally sourced seaweed. He'd be happy, and maybe even thankful to have gone through his current heartbreak, as it had brought him to a better future.

And me—most likely I'd be back in LA, paying half the rent somewhere with my sister and niece while we saved up for a house of our own. I didn't begrudge my sister this plan since I owed everything to Tory, but there were times I wished I could choose to do anything I wanted.

As far as dreams went, becoming an esthetician might not seem ambitious. But then again, I'd be so content to work for the joy of a chosen profession instead of being constrained to chase the money.

We boarded the flight, and I was quick to realize business-class travel on an Emirates flight was a whole new level.

"Sorry, first class was booked," Reid apologized while placing both of our bags in the overhead carry-on bin.

"Oh, yeah, this business class is seriously roughing it." I took my seat, smelling the rich leather and stretching my long legs out in front of me.

He sat down in the chair beside me. "The A380 is a nice plane with these newer business-class cabins." He went on about the model of the plane, giving details from the engine to the upgrades before suddenly stopping. "Sorry, nerd alert."

"I found it fascinating."

He chuckled. "Sure you did."

"No, actually I did. It eases my anxiety to hear this plane is new. Now then, what kind of movies do we get to choose from?" I picked up the remote and pressed the on button for the flat-screen television in front of me.

"Aren't you planning to sleep?"

It was a sixteen-and-a-half-hour flight from Dubai to Fort Lauderdale, Florida. From there, we'd transfer to a three-and-a-half-hour flight to the Turks and Caicos.

"Yeah, I'll get some sleep at some point." But currently I was a kid in a candy store as I perused all of the movie options.

As the loading of the plane continued, the flight attendant appeared, dressed impeccably in her uniform and wearing a perfect smile which didn't hint at the early morning hour or that we were about to be trapped together in this thing for the next sixteen hours.

"Good morning and welcome. Can I offer you anything to drink before we take off?"

Reid deferred to me, always the gentleman.

"Um, ice water would be great," I said.

"Make it two ice waters, please," he requested, and the attendant went to fetch our drinks.

"She was pretty, nice British accent." All this talk about my type of guy had me wondering what was Reid's type of woman—aside from his ex.

He thumbed through his magazine. "Was she? I didn't notice."

I chuckled. "That's a great boyfriend response."

He flashed a grin and took my hand, kissing the inside of my wrist in an unexpected and intimate gesture. The touch of his lips against my skin sent shivers racing down to my toes.

"From here on out, you're stuck with me."

"Yep." My mouth popped the p on the word as I took my hand back and tried to fight the butterflies in my stomach. My eyes automatically tracked forward toward the open door. It represented my last chance to escape this journey to heartbreak.

But luckily, the flight attendant returned just in time, distracting me from my worry over spending the next few days with Reid. She brought our drinks and little white ramekins of warmed nuts. Nothing convinced me to stay and see this thing through like warmed, salted nuts. I let out a resigned sigh. Perhaps they were "calming nuts."

"You okay?" Reid asked, causing us both to laugh. We were in grave danger of wearing out that particular question.

"New plan. We need a code word or phrase, so we won't have to use those words all weekend."

"Hm." He sipped his water. "How about, are you thirsty?"

"But what if I happen to be thirsty?"

His grin brought out his dimple. Oh, dimples, how I love thee.

"How about, could you use a cocktail?"

"Given the circumstances of this weekend, the answer will always be yes. How about, do you want some warm nuts?" What could I say? My creativity was limited to the snack in front of me.

"Could make for some funny looks. I like it. So then, how are your warm nuts?"

A giggle escaped my throat at the absurdity of our little inside phrase. "My warm nuts are incredible. I'm digging business-class service already."

"You're a cheap date if the nuts are doing it for you."

I picked up the menu on the center console. "I doubt these seats were cheap. By the way, thank you for the flight to California afterwards." It couldn't have been cheap either. Although I was aware he had a good deal of family money and probably made a good living as a security director, I would never take his generosity for granted.

"It was the least I could do to offset the discomfort you're about to experience."

"Guess I'd better fasten my seat belt." Both figuratively and literally.

AFTER A LARGE BREAKFAST OF PANCAKES, bacon, and fruit—in business class they actually served you on real plates with silverware—I gave up trying to watch another movie and settled in for sleep. The beauty of these seats was you could lay them flat like a bed. But the bed aspect made me very aware I'd be sleeping next to Reid.

Guess I ought to get used to it since we'd be sharing a

room tonight. But wait? Would we be sharing a bed too? I hadn't thought to ask. I finally fell asleep dreaming about warm nuts.

I woke, stretched out the kinks, and glanced at my phone, which told me I'd slept six hours. The plane was relatively quiet and dark, with a melodic white noise humming in my ears from the jet engines. As I sat up, I realized most of the passengers were sleeping, including my seatmate. I swallowed hard at the sight of his baby face, completely relaxed in slumber. Couldn't he at least snore or drool or do something unattractive? Then again, if he had, I'd probably make an exception and find the flaw as sexy as the rest of him.

As if he could hear my internal thoughts, he stretched—adorably, of course—and opened his eyes. Immediately, he focused on me. "Hi," came his gravelly morning voice.

"Hi." Why was his morning voice sexy while mine sounded as if I'd chain-smoked a pack of cigarettes?

"How long did you sleep?"

"Six hours. I just woke up."

"Mm, you're excited for another movie, aren't you?"

Before succumbing to sleep, I'd rattled off to him the titles of at least a dozen movies I couldn't wait to watch, so yeah, I was eager. Considering I'd never had cable television and didn't frequently have a chance to watch movies, was it any wonder I was enthusiastic?

"I am. But first I need to use the lavatory." While Reid probably had perfect morning breath, I knew, without a doubt, I did not.

"Let me get your bag."

He was so considerate, setting his seat to the upright position and climbing out so he could fetch my bag out of the overhead.

"Thank you," I murmured, taking my toiletry bag. I made my way to the bathroom and, once in the closet-like space, checked my hair in the mirror. I was happy to see it had stayed calm. If I'd left it curly, it would've been a mess by now. I took a good ten minutes to wash my face, brush my teeth, and freshen up before returning to my seat. Once there, I smiled at my seatmate, who appeared as though he'd also freshened up and was now sitting up in his chair. Our bedding had already been folded.

"The flight attendant will be back with some sandwiches and drinks if you're hungry."

I was.

Once we arrived in Fort Lauderdale, we went through customs and then straight to the Emirates arrivals lounge. There I was able to take a shower and change into expensive outfit number one. It consisted of a soft yellow-and-white sundress with tan espadrille wedge shoes. I accessorized with a simple silver chain bracelet and my silver locket, the one holding a picture of my niece.

When I came out of the women's lounge, Reid was waiting on me, leaned up against the wall. He'd changed into khaki pants and a baby-blue, short-sleeved dress shirt. He resembled the pre-breakup, fresh-faced Reid. When he smiled, I noted how clear his eyes were and how healthily his skin glowed.

"Hi," I said, enjoying the way his eyes lit up at my appearance.

"Hi. You look beautiful."

Never comfortable with compliments, I deflected. "It's the straight hair. Makes a difference."

He cocked his head to the side and was about to speak, but we were interrupted by an airline employee who'd walked up. "Sir, madam, your gate has been announced." She went on to give us directions to the gate and to wish us a good flight.

We walked down the wide concourse toward our gate, weaving in and out between fellow passengers. In front of a convenience store, Reid stopped and handed me his carry-on suitcase. "Can you watch this while I get a few things? And do you want anything yourself?"

"No, I'm good, thanks."

A few minutes later, he came out with a plastic bag.

"What did you get?"

He dug inside and fished out a box which he then handed to me. "Candy for you, milady. Jolly Ranchers are your favorite, right?"

It was sweet. I couldn't believe he'd remembered. But then, of course he had. We wouldn't be able to pull this off if he didn't remember such things. I murmured a thank you for his thoughtfulness and almost couldn't wait until we'd boarded the next flight before popping an apple-flavored candy into my mouth.

"How are the nuts?" he asked after I let out a long sigh.

Our code question immediately made me smile. "Good. Yours?"

He bit his lip to keep from laughing. "Doing okay."

But four hours later, I was definitely not doing okay when the cab pulled up to a massive beachside resort. The entrance was lined with palm trees that looked picture perfect in the early afternoon. White columns and impressive archways led to a spectacular, marbled lobby inside. Were they piping in bird sounds, or were those real birds chirping? And was that the scent of tropical flowers, or did they Febreze the place every few minutes? In addition to all this, there was a large water fountain right in the center of the lobby.

Holy out of my league.

The place looked like something from a movie scene, complete with staff in impeccable tan uniforms and megawatt welcome-to-vacation smiles who took our bags. We were officially in paradise. I jumped when Reid took my hand in his.

"Your nuts holding up okay?" he whispered.

"Yeah. Of course. I was momentarily awestruck by this place. Not playing my part very well."

He squeezed my hand. "How many times do I have to tell you to just be yourself?"

His words indicated one thing but his actions quite another. Hadn't he bought me all these designer clothes? But I just smiled. It wasn't his fault I was out of my element.

We walked in and headed straight for the front desk. I noticed Reid was on edge, his eyes darting around the lobby. I imagined he was wondering who might be about to walk up to him, friend or foe. What a strange feeling that must be. No wonder he hadn't wanted to deal with it alone. I was genuinely glad to be here for him.

He kept his hand in mine at the front desk, bringing my knuckles up to his lips to brush them with a kiss.

This is all pretend. This is all pretend.

"There are two women staring at us from the floor above." The lobby was open and airy, with steps leading up to a bar or restaurant on the second level that gave views of the water fountain below. "By the way they're gawking, I assume they must know you, but neither of them is your ex."

To his credit, Reid didn't so much as flick a glance their way. Instead, he smoothed an invisible hair behind my ear and bent his head closer.

"You okay with me kissing you?" he asked in a whisper.

"Stop asking and kiss me already," I ground out. While he

was only putting on a show, my body was already tingling with very real anticipation.

He chuckled, amusement dancing in his eyes. "You're right. I'll stop asking." But instead of dropping his lips to mine, he went for my neck, kissing me below my ear.

A shiver snaked through my entire body.

Move over, warm airplane nuts. Neck kisses were now my official kryptonite.

The clerk handed over the card keys. "Enjoy your stay, Mr. and Mrs. Maxwell," he said in a thick accent.

While I blushed, Reid gave me a wink and didn't bother to correct the clerk's mistake in assuming I was his wife.

"Ramone will take your luggage and show you to your room."

"Thank you." Reid then took my hand as we followed the luggage cart.

Once we were inside the hotel room, I experienced another few moments of awe. Marble tiles led into a living room that was larger than my apartment. All of the plush furnishings and paint appeared new. New and expensive. From the flat-screen television to the fully stocked bar in the corner, the room was high class. Off to the right of the main room was a large bedroom with an en-suite bathroom showcasing a Jacuzzi tub the size of a small car. But the balconies, one off the bedroom and another off the living room, were what truly stole the show.

"Holy shit," I exclaimed, opening the sliding door. I walked out to take in the view of the gorgeous white-sand beach and turquoise-blue water. Inhaling, I caught the wonderful smell of what I instantly dubbed "island air," something scented with the ocean and all things vacation.

Reid thanked the bellhop and handed him a tip before joining me.

Here I'd thought Dubai had beautiful beaches. "It's gorgeous," I breathed.

"It is. So about the bed—"

My eyes swung into the bedroom and focused on the large king-sized bed. Gulp. "Yeah?"

"I thought it might be odd to ask for two doubles."

"Yes. It would."

"I can take the couch."

My gaze tracked toward the ornamental sofa. It appeared uncomfortable for sleeping and undoubtedly wouldn't fit his six-foot-something frame. "I don't mind sharing the bed."

He grinned. "I promise to stay on my side."

How practical. How disappointing.

"Are you hungry? You want to go get some lunch? Or would you rather rest? You could take a nap, and I could go downstairs to give you some privacy."

I rolled my eyes. "Would you give your new girlfriend privacy after stepping into this beautiful room with the romantic view? No, if we were actually dating we'd be fu—" I was about to say fucking like bunnies, but stopped. "We'd be, uh, busy with each other."

His cheeks stained pink, but he chuckled. "We'd be fu-nning? Is that what you were about to say?"

"Yep. We'd be funning." Jesus, now I was blushing. "But I am hungry."

"I think room service should fit our fu-n image."

Here was hoping I could now get my mind off of all the fu-n ways we could have been spending our time.

Chapter Twenty-One
REID

My gaze was riveted on Teagan, who sat on the hotel couch taking the biggest bite known to man of her club sandwich. She then let out a groan that could provide the soundtrack for an erotic movie.

"God, this is delicious."

As I sat in a chair across from her, I snapped myself out of my newest fascination, watching her eat, and took a bite of my own hamburger. "It is good."

She approached food as she did everything else. Unapologetically. She didn't whine about the calories in the fries or pick at the sandwich. She took a big ol' bite and enjoyed the flavors, knowing she'd hit the gym extra hard the next time without any regrets. It was not only refreshing, but also sexy as hell.

"So what's on the agenda tonight?" she asked in between bites.

"Cocktails for a welcome reception at five. After that, I guess we'll figure out what to do on our own for dinner." Oddly, I didn't dread having to see Vanessa or my mother as much as I'd thought I would. It must be the effect of the woman sitting across from me, currently shoving fries into her mouth.

She wiped at some mayo on her chin. "Gives us a couple hours. I may take a dip in the bathtub that's the size of my entire bathroom."

"Knock yourself out. I'm going to unpack. You want me to unpack you too?"

"You're unpacking your suitcase?"

"Let me guess. You're one of those people who prefers to pick your stuff out of the suitcase."

"Well, yeah. Although normally I only travel home to see my sister, so it's nothing fancier than T-shirts and jeans. I'll hang my stuff later."

As soon as I heard the water shut off from the tub, I closed my eyes and took a deep breath. Imagining her getting into the bath was sheer, utter torment. If we were a real couple, I'd take her a glass of wine, or maybe she'd prefer a martini.

Teagan came out of the bathroom twenty minutes later, looking fresh and rosy from her bath. She was dressed in yoga pants and a T-shirt and appeared completely unaware of just how attractive she was. Some women spent hours putting on makeup, yet she was naturally gorgeous without.

"My turn for a shower." I'd need a cold one at this rate.

Turned out the cold shower was only a temporary fix. Because ninety minutes later she came out of the bedroom looking absolutely gorgeous in her little black cocktail dress with her hair down, her makeup on, and a smile firmly in place.

Faking it had just gotten a lot more real.

WE WERE on our way to the cocktail party when we both spotted a tent off the terrace with a line leading up to it.

"What do you think it is?" Teagan whispered.

"Not sure, but let's check it out." It was clear there were other wedding guests in the line since they were dressed similarly to us.

After a quick question, we found out the line was for a psychic reading inside the tent.

"You game?" I asked her, curious about something I'd never explored.

"Are you?"

"Yeah, a psychic could be fun."

"Mm." She didn't look convinced.

"You aren't freaked out by it, are you?"

"To be honest, the supernatural, unexplained things like psychics, mediums, and magicians—it all gives me the creeps. I'm more of a lay-it-out-for-me kind of girl. I'm not big on surprises or smoke and mirrors."

"Same, but live a little." I wasn't the type who believed in this kind of thing either, but if I was stepping out of my comfort zone and moving on from Vanessa, perhaps the psychic tent was a sign I should try something else that was new.

"Okay. Let's see what crazy predictions she may have."

Finally, it was our turn, and we stepped inside the tent. Sitting at a table inside was a small woman with brown, weathered skin. She was anywhere between seventy and a hundred years old. A colorful headdress matched her embroidered, loose-fitting blouse.

"Come in and take a seat," she said with an islander accent.

The tent was filled with bright-colored tapestries and

blankets that hung from floor to ceiling, giving the small space the desired ambiance for a psychic reading.

Teagan whispered, "What do you want to bet the bride and your ex slipped her a twenty to tell me I'm doomed?"

I grinned and was about to reassure her when the woman spoke.

"I do not take bribes. This is serious work. My name is Imelda, and I've been a psychic for over fifty years."

Teagan sucked in a breath. "Sorry. Bad joke."

I started to chuckle, but Imelda's glare shut me up.

"She hates us both," I murmured under my breath as we both took seats.

Now that I was closer, I could see the table was covered with a printed cloth and adorned with lighted candles, books, and beads. Whether all of this was functional or aesthetic, I wasn't sure, but it definitely set the mood. The same could be said of the vanilla spiced incense permeating the room.

"Give me your hands."

I could sense Teagan's hesitation, so I took our hands, still clasped, and put them on the table.

Imelda put her old, weathered hands on top of ours and closed her eyes.

I winked at my date who appeared as though she was ready to bolt.

"I see a sexual spark between the two of you. A definite chemistry."

"She can't keep her hands off of me."

My quip was meant to be funny, but it earned me a stern glare from Imelda.

Teagan's lips twitched with the hint of a smile.

Imelda's gravelly voice spoke again. "I see a much brighter spark with her than with you."

Teagan smirked. "He does tend to lie there a lot while I do all the work."

The vision of her on top of me made me suck in a breath. Guaranteed she wouldn't be the one doing all the work.

Imelda narrowed her eyes, looking at us both. "You two haven't had intercourse yet, have you?"

Her scrutiny had me squirming in my seat. "What makes you say that?"

"Because of all the unsatisfied sexual energy between the two of you."

Gulp. I didn't dare glance at Teagan.

Imelda leaned forward. "Don't take things too slow. This is your window. I see a long and happy future for the two of you."

Double gulp.

She then let go of my hand and concentrated on Teagan, whose eyes went wide.

"My dear, you are loyal, but the numbers of those you trust are small. You crave options in your life, don't you?"

Teagan cleared her voice. "Yes."

I was fascinated with her reading, but even more so with Teagan's confirmation.

"You will be tested over the next few days in ways you won't expect."

Teagan nodded.

Imelda then motioned for my hand again. Taking it into hers, she breathed deeply. "You need to let go of the toxic people in your past."

I would imagine most people who came into her tent could relate to this advice, but her next words really got my attention for some reason.

"Your past may try to trap you. Don't let it."

Well, that was cryptic.

She suddenly took hold of both of our hands, meeting my eyes. "You will have to make the first move with this one. She won't ever tell you, but she's shy."

Whoa. That one was way off base.

Suddenly, she let go of both our hands. "Have a good night, my friends."

In other words, she had others to get to. I slipped her a twenty-dollar bill. "Thank you for the reading."

"It was my pleasure."

Teagan and I didn't speak until we were outside, away from Imelda and the long line of people now forming to see her.

"So, that was interesting."

She expelled a long breath. "Yeah. She must throw spaghetti against the wall in hopes something sticks."

"Right, like the thing about you being shy. Obviously, that's not true." I could totally see Teagan making the first move when it came to a man. There wasn't a timid bone in her body.

"Yep. Me, shy? Can you imagine?"

Yet she didn't sound convincing, which made me pause. Could it be possible she actually was shy when it came to making the first move with a man?

"I have to admit, the fact she knew I like options was creepy."

"And it's something I hadn't guessed. Why do you enjoy options?" Getting to know Teagan was like discovering a small thread you could pull on in order to unravel a string of more information.

"When I was little, I didn't get to choose what I ate for meals, what clothes I wore, or even whether or not I wanted to go into foster care. So I suppose having options, even if they're small ones, gives me comfort. I know I get to make a decision instead of having no choice."

What she said made sense. Her unpredictable childhood with a drug addict mother must have given her very few choices.

"Sorry, it's stupid."

My voice was thick with an emotion I didn't want to name. "I don't think it's stupid at all." I recalled the way her face had lit up at the number of movies available and the various menu options on the flight. No wonder she'd been so happy.

Chapter Twenty-Two
TEAGAN

We walked hand in hand into the hotel ballroom for the cocktail party. Reid was dressed in a charcoal gray suit with a light blue shirt that matched his eyes. The outfit seemed rather formal for a beach wedding, but then again, what did I know? Perhaps wearing a formal suit and tie in eighty-degree weather by the beach was fun.

Fun, like having a psychic hit the nail on the head when it came to my childhood emotional scar. Sure, she could've guessed how much I liked options and gotten lucky, but I didn't think so. All of what she'd said about me had been eerily accurate, except, of course, her comment about the pent-up sexual energy between us. Or perhaps I had enough for us both, setting her meter off target.

"Something from the bar?" I offered, trying not to sound desperate for some liquid courage. It was game time, and eyes were already on us. I sincerely hoped I didn't cause him to regret his decision to bring me here as his fake girlfriend.

"Yes, but let me get the drinks. You prefer Sex on the Beach or in the Driveway?"

My laugh was instantaneous, and his humor was what I'd

needed to break the tension. The fact he remembered my home blender drink of choice was impressive. "It's a beach wedding, so let's stick with doing it on the beach for now, but do me a favor and don't get trapped by your past. Not until after I have a drink in my hand."

His lips curved up in a sexy grin. "I'll see what I can do."

After he left, I wandered to a nearby high-top cocktail table to wait for him. I'd just taken a meatball from a waiter's tray when a glossy brunette with a blond sidekick came up. I recognized them both as the two women on the balcony when we'd checked in.

Mean girl alert. After all the years in middle and high school bullied by rich, spoiled, bitchy girls, I could practically smell it on them.

The brunette spoke first. "Hi, I'm the bride, Jamie, and this is my maid of honor, Tiffany."

After an awkward pause where I cursed the damn meatball in my mouth, I managed a smile despite wishing I could tell them to get lost. But this was the dance. The type which began with polite conversation before morphing into passive-aggressive, followed by just plain mean.

Finally I was able to swallow and speak. "Nice to meet you both. I'm Teagan."

First up for catty bitch of the year was the maid of honor, the blonde. "Right, you're Reid's little rebound."

And so went the dance.

"I prefer to be called girlfriend, but the Reid part is true."

Jamie, not to be outdone in the bitchiest-girl contest, took her shot. "I saw you in the lobby checking in earlier and thought there's no way she's Reid's date, but you look prettier tonight. Guess it must've been bad lighting."

Mean girls gonna hate. "Yeah, come to think of it, I spotted you on the balcony, but you looked much more knocked up then, so I didn't even recognize you tonight. God bless good lighting, am I right?"

I had the satisfaction of seeing her insincere smile drop like a rock. I might be here as Reid's fake girlfriend, but I certainly didn't have to fake being nice to shitty people.

"I'd say it was a pleasure to meet you, but—"

"It would be a lie. Believe me. Same. Ah, here's my boyfriend now. Reid, you know the bride and her maid of honor, I presume?"

He flashed a charming smile. "I do. Nice to see you, Jamie and Tiffany."

"Yes, nice to see you too, Reid. I still can't believe you called up last minute to ask to bring a date. It's bad form. And after meeting her, I wish you had better taste."

Was it wrong to slap a pregnant lady? All signs pointed to yes. But what if it was only a little bop on the forehead in order to insult her? Or hell, I'd settle for slapping the maid of honor as her proxy.

I half expected my fake boyfriend to give me a disapproving frown, but much to my surprise, he put his arm around my waist, hauling me close to him. "I'd say my taste has definitely improved for the better. Take care, ladies."

I let out a breath once they turned and left, meeting Reid's amused eyes.

"Not playing well with the others already?"

"Petty mean girls. I realize the bride is your ex's cousin, but damn—they came in hot."

"And judging from the looks of it, they're leaving to lick their wounds. I'm sorry you had to deal with that."

"Eh. Mean girls are all over the place. They don't bother me anymore."

Leave it to him to catch my slip. "But they used to?"

"No, I didn't mean—"

He wasn't letting it go. "Yes you did, and it's only us. Tell me the truth."

"Haven't we had enough sharing for the evening?" Imelda had been quite sufficient for me.

"All right, I'll guess. You lived in foster care in an affluent area, which meant you probably didn't fit in."

I should've expected his perception.

"Let's just say ill-fitting, hand-me-down clothes coupled with my red hair and pale skin made me an easy target for mean girls in school."

He leaned in to whisper in my ear. "Yet look at you now. Stunning and confident."

"Dressed in designer clothes." Lest he forget I was still a poor girl without the proper wardrobe for the weekend.

He shook his head. "You could be wearing anything and remain the sexiest woman in the room."

His unexpected compliment added to my perpetual emotional confusion. There was no one around. No reason for him to say these words unless he'd wanted to. As I was about to say something to change the subject, I watched him stiffen and followed his gaze.

Walking toward us was an attractive-looking, older woman dressed to impress in a gorgeous silver cocktail dress.

"Who is she?"

"My mother."

Damn. How could two words be so utterly terrifying? Maybe it was because I had little experience dealing with parents. I'd never known my father, and my mother wasn't the type to actually give a shit. My foster parents had only been in the picture for a few months and had been overwhelmed with other kids. And my high school boyfriend had been too ashamed of me to ever introduce me to his rich parents.

Knowing it was pointless to let old insecurities threaten my mood, I silenced them.

"You meant it when you said you're not close with your mom, right?" I needed a quick confirmation since the first impressions I gave were normally for shit. This pending meeting warranted a big swig of my drink.

"No, I'm not. But she's never noticed. Here she comes. Act like you're in love with me."

"Sex on the Beach" suddenly became "Sex Stuck in my Throat" as I started to cough uncontrollably.

"Jesus, you okay?" Reid asked, concern etched on his face as he pounded me on the back.

"Yep. God, this is embarrassing." A few people were staring, and my eyes were watering, most likely creating a hot mess of my mascara.

But he only grinned, taking my hand and kissing the inside of the wrist in a surprisingly tender gesture. "That should teach you to take things slower. Enjoy the taste a little more before swallowing."

I stared at him, his words having sparked an unexpected pang of lust. "Wh-what?"

He rolled his eyes, his smirk firmly in place. "Get your mind out of the gutter. And don't go and choke to death the first night. It would be embarrassing for us both. Also, incoming."

Shit. Yes it was. Mrs. Maxwell in the flesh.

"Darling, it's been forever."

She kissed her son on both cheeks in a fancy greeting I'd only ever seen in movies.

"Hello, Mother."

Her hand held his chin. "The breakup doesn't look good on you, my boy. But nothing a good spa day and a reconciliation can't cure."

He sighed, stepping out of her touch. "On the contrary, I've never felt better. Mother, this is my girlfriend, Teagan Larson. Teagan, this is my mother, Clarissa Maxwell."

I was about to say it was nice to meet her too, but she pretended I didn't exist, focusing solely on Reid. "I prefer to go by my maiden name these days, Clarissa Chandler."

She finally turned a slow gaze to focus on me.

Guess I was up. "Nice to meet you, Ms. Chandler."

Her eyes raked down my dress to my shoes, clearly assessing exactly what I was wearing and if I was worthy. By the time she made it back up to my face, I lifted a brow, schooling my features to bored indifference. I hated the small amount of self-doubt that hit me under her scrutiny. Guess I now understood why Reid had dropped thousands on a suitable wardrobe for me.

"Be a dear and fetch your mother a drink, Reid. Gin martini, splash of vermouth, two olives, dirty."

Jesus, even her drink order was fancy.

Reid's glance toward me asked if I was okay being left alone with her.

I flashed him a brave smile. I had this. Maybe.

"I'll be right back."

I drained the rest of my drink, wishing it was a shot to soothe my nerves. But I wouldn't give Reid's mother the satisfaction of recognizing how anxious I was. I also wouldn't be the one to initiate conversation as if I craved her approval.

"Reid hasn't once mentioned you. Where are you from?"

"Originally from Los Angeles, but I'm currently living in Dubai."

She rolled her eyes. "Both places are deserts with absolutely no history worth knowing about. I suppose you went to college in California too."

Imagine if she knew I only had a GED. It was tempting to say fuck it and tell her the truth, but I wouldn't embarrass Reid that way. "Yes, I went to UCLA."

She sighed as if put off by the thought I'd attended a public university. "And your family? What do they do?"

"My mother and father passed away when I was younger. They were both in pharmaceuticals." Neither of these were entirely lies. I assumed my father had been a drug addict like my mother, and both of them could easily be deceased.

I breathed a sigh of relief when Reid started walking our way, drinks in hand. But his mother wasn't done.

"You're appealing in a wild and unrefined way, my dear, but I should warn you. Reid always finds his way back to Vanessa. She has enviable genetics, deep family roots, and an impeccable upbringing."

"You make her sound like a prize cocker spaniel."

She smiled, the action not meeting her eyes. "There's a lot to be said for pedigree. And to be clear. He'll grow tired of you, same as he tired of all the other in-between girls. I would hate to see you get your feelings hurt."

Yeah, I bet. I managed to keep my facial expression neutral even as her words hit home. Hadn't Reid suggested the same thing? He didn't want to risk another relationship right now. He'd inadvertently hurt a woman the last time he'd gotten involved with someone new after breaking up with Vanessa. "Your concern is touching."

She shrugged, turning to Reid who'd arrived in time to hear my last words.

I took the drink from his hand before he had a chance to set it on the table.

"I always try to do right by my two boys. Now then, Reid, have you spoken with Chance yet?"

"No, we aren't speaking at the moment." He slipped his

mother's martini on the table before landing a kiss on my cheek.

"You two are brothers and the only siblings you each have."

"Actually, we have six other half-siblings courtesy of your first husband."

Her heavily botoxed face might have been frowning. "They hardly count. That you would bring them up displeases me. Chance will be here for the weekend, so you should take the opportunity to make up."

The news settled like a pit in my stomach. I knew Chance's presence would make this weekend much more uncomfortable for Reid.

"We're not making up, Mother. What he did is unforgivable," Reid said between clenched teeth.

"Nothing is unforgivable when it comes to family. Now then, I'm off to catch up with Vanessa's parents. After all, we both want to see you two back together where you belong."

My date appeared as though he needed a stiff drink.

As soon as she left, I leaned over to whisper, "So, I think your mom really likes me."

He burst out laughing. "I'd be worried if she actually did. Don't take it personally—she doesn't like me much either. What did she say to you?"

"Something about a cocker spaniel, and me living in the desert with no history. To be honest, I was too busy waiting on the next drink to pay too much attention."

He shook his head. "Let me apologize, both for her words and for what you're about to endure this entire weekend. It's bound to suck."

I lifted my glass to his. "Here's to sucking."

He clinked his glass of bourbon to mine. "So long as it's not on any part of my brother."

Dammit. My drink hit my throat wrong, and bam, I was coughing again.

But Reid was on it, taking my drink from my hand and patting my back gently. His expression was apologetic. "Sorry, did I go too far?"

"Hi, have we met? No, you didn't go too far. Just unexpected humor, I can appreciate, even if my drink does not."

His smile was the type that kicked me straight in the gut. Intimate, sincere, and focused on me. Suddenly, all the blood was rushing to my head.

"Are your nuts still warm and toasty?"

I needed to get myself together and remember what this was. A pretense. "Yeah, I'm good now."

We talked some more over appetizers and drinks until two guys came up. Reid introduced them as Kevin and Chris, one was the groom-to-be and another groomsman.

"Nice to meet you." I shook both their outstretched hands. Both seemed nice but kept giving me looks as if they were weirded out to see someone new with their friend.

Suddenly Kevin winced. "We're being beckoned for pictures. You don't mind if we steal your date, do you, Teagan?"

"Not at all."

But Reid took my hand. "Do you want to come out on the patio and watch?"

Watch him be photographed with his ex-fiancée? Having a root canal sounded more fun. "Sure. I'll swing by the bar again and join you soon."

I needed something stronger than my current cocktail to get through the night. I hold my own, but alcohol certainly helped in the endeavor. The designer dress, high-fashion shoes, and fake pedigree were all starting to wear on me, and this was only the first night.

What I needed was whiskey. It would either be a good or a bad idea as it did tend to fuel my feistiness. But of all situations, this one merited at least one glass.

"Rye whiskey neat," I ordered from the bartender. While watching him pour, I sensed someone come up beside me.

"Reid drinks bourbon, not rye whiskey," came the masculine voice.

I tipped the bartender for a generous pour and didn't bother to make eye contact with the unwelcome intruder. "Who says this is for Reid?" I took a sip and intended to walk away, but the stranger wasn't done with the conversation.

"Interesting. I would've pegged you as a Cosmo or vodka cranberry type of girl."

My side glance took in the expensive threads before traveling up to the handsome face they belonged to. There was a familiarity I couldn't quite place. I pasted on a smile, figuring he was just another rich bastard here for the wedding. "And what would give you that idea?"

He shrugged. "A fruity drink tends to go with the Jimmy Choos and Prada purse."

I didn't miss the disdain in his tone. "Ah, says the guy wearing a three-thousand-dollar suit. Let me guess. You're a Scotch guy."

"Four-thousand-dollar suit, and no, I'll have a bourbon, neat. Blanton's if you have it," he directed toward the bartender.

The bartender was quick to produce a bottle from the cabinet and gave another generous pour. "Here you are, Mr. Maxwell."

Maxwell. Ah, this had to be the infamous older brother.

"I propose a toast." He turned fully to face me and held up his drink.

The similarity to Reid was there in his eyes, nose, and full lips. Yet while Reid had a youthfulness in his face and kind eyes, Chance was definitely sharper in his features and harder in his edges. Rather than the freshly shaved and neat look Reid sported, his brother wore a five o'clock shadow.

My brow lifted along with the veil of pretense. This wasn't a guy on whom I needed to waste any fake niceties. "A toast to what, pray tell?"

"How about to you being the rebound girl?"

At least his insult wasn't wrapped in a fake smile. Just pure asshole laid out there for all. I held up my glass and clinked it against his. "How perfectly unoriginal. I have to say, having heard your reputation, Chance, I expected more from you."

His jaw tic was immensely satisfying.

"You know, for a guy who went to all the trouble of breaking up Reid and Vanessa, I would guess you'd be happier to see me here."

"Assuming you aren't the same type?"

A humorless laugh was my response and I leaned in, so only he could hear me. "Don't let the designer dress and overpriced shoes fool you. I'm nothing like Vanessa. For instance, I haven't once thought of sucking your dick, and it's been a whole two minutes."

I slammed back the rest of my whiskey before giving him one last satisfied smirk and walking off.

Fuck him and the rest of this crowd. Jesus, was it any wonder Reid had moved to the other side of the world? After twenty minutes with these pretentious jerks, I didn't blame him.

As I walked out to the terrace, my eyes found my date immediately in the group of men currently posing for a photographer. Over to the side were several women waiting their turn to join them. It took only a moment to find Vanessa.

She looked similar to when I'd seen her last year in Dubai. As much as I'd have loved to mentally pick apart her appearance, I couldn't. She was stunning in a strapless black-and-white dress, her makeup was flawless, and her long blond hair flowed straight down her back. Whereas I was tall and curvy, she was petite and slender. If glamorous Barbie could come to life, Reid's ex is what she'd look like, right down to the perfectly whitened teeth.

She was standing next to the bride and another bridesmaid. They were all staring over my way without disguising their disdain. Damn. I should've grabbed another drink to have in hand.

Despite their gaping, I didn't bother to avert my eyes. It wasn't my style to be intimidated or insecure in the face of scrutiny. Hell, over the years I'd perfected indifference.

"Hi, are you Teagan?" A voice from my left side belonged to a woman who appeared to be about my age. She had a kind expression and big brown eyes.

A friendly smile. Oh, how I'd missed thee. "Yes, I am."

"I'm Ellen, Phil's wife."

The nice people Reid had mentioned. "It's great to meet you."

"You too. When Phil told me you'd be here, I was so relieved. Without you, I feared I'd be standing to the side like this a lot this weekend, all by myself."

"Thank you for coming over here. It's nice to see a friendly smile." Ellen was adorable with her heart-shaped face and stunning olive skin.

She glanced toward the bride's wedding party. "Believe me. Same."

When the photographer called the group of women over to stand with the men, my eyes tracked Reid to gauge his first reaction to his ex. The stiff shoulders, the set jaw—I could practically feel the tension rolling off of him. Especially when they positioned Vanessa next to him.

Was there any question who he'd be paired up with to walk down the aisle? Unbelievable, though it really wasn't unexpected given the bride was cousin to the woman who wanted him back.

I noted Vanessa's gloating smile pointed in my direction as she conversed with my man.

My man? That was the whiskey talking. But he was my man as far as anyone else knew. As if sensing my annoyance, Ellen spoke again.

"I don't know how you're doing it. This weekend is bound to be hell for you."

My eyes collided with Reid's, and my smirk said "remember you're my date for the weekend."

I forced myself to relax my shoulders. "I'm sure making my weekend hell is her plan."

"Just keep in mind who he's sleeping with tonight. It won't be her."

Ellen had more conviction than I did.

Chapter Twenty-Three
REID

As I was posing for pictures with the groom's side of the wedding party, I suddenly felt caught in the crosshairs of a familiar gaze. How many minutes over the years had I wasted searching Vanessa out in a crowd? From the time I fell in love with her in middle school and through all of the years we'd spent dating, she'd always been the center of my entire world. Maybe that was at the crux of why we'd ultimately failed. Because we'd both always put her first.

Upon seeing her, I braced myself for an impact. But the moment our gazes met, the anticipated jolt wasn't there. The sting of pride was present, but even that was a dull ache instead of the sharp pain I'd expected.

As soon as the photographer called the women over for the next round of photos, she came up with a big smile. "Hi, Reid, how are you?"

"Fine, thanks. How are you?" I could do this. I could have a civilized conversation with my ex.

She looked around as if she desired privacy, but there was

none to be found. All eyes were on us. "I'm okay. But I was hurt to hear you brought a date. Who is she?"

"She's someone I work with."

"How long have you been together?"

Her question hit me with déjà vu. It's what she'd asked when I'd been dating Shelly years ago. And I was ashamed to remember my answer had been, "not long enough to be serious." I'd purposefully left the door open, not realizing how serious it had been for Shelly at the time. Even after all these years, I felt terrible that I'd gone home the same night to break things off so I could reconcile with Vanessa. But this was different. I had no desire to take Vanessa back.

"A few weeks." Over Vanessa's shoulder, a vision of red hair caught my eye. Teagan wore a smirk on her face, making me want to walk over and ask what was on her mind.

"We should get in position for pictures."

Vanessa didn't appear happy with my suggestion or the fact I was already turning to go. "We need to talk. Please give me a few minutes. We can meet tonight. Get some closure."

I didn't want to talk to her later, but neither did I want a scene in front of everyone. By the way her eyes were tearing up, that's exactly what was going to happen if I didn't agree to meet her.

"Fine. We can talk tonight."

Her beautiful face morphed into a triumphant smile. One I'd seen too many times to count. "I need your number."

I hated the fact Teagan was witnessing Vanessa pull out her phone to type in the digits I relayed to her. It felt like a step back instead of demonstrating that I was over her.

Thirty minutes later, the bridal party was getting restless. How many pictures did they need for a cocktail party two nights before the actual wedding? The answer was too many.

Especially since Vanessa insisted on standing next to me for every snap. Because I didn't want to cause a scene, I kept my mouth shut, but after the last shot, I walked over to where Teagan was standing beside Ellen.

"Hi," I whispered, cupping her chin. Faking it was feeling, oh, so real.

"Hi." She barely got a chance to respond before my lips descended. The kiss was soft, chaste by all standards, yet it also felt incredibly intimate.

I leaned in close to her ear. "I taste whiskey on your lips. Should I be concerned?"

A giggle bubbled up in her throat. "Not yet. Unfortunately, I met your brother. I was hoping your mom was wrong, and he wouldn't be here."

"Chance rarely does what's expected of him. Did he say anything to you?"

"Yeah, some shit about bourbon being better than rye whiskey."

I had a feeling she was omitting a great deal of the conversation, but I appreciated that she was intent on keeping me calm.

"I don't understand why he's here. He hates weddings."

"I would guess he's here to talk to you. Maybe to apologize."

I expelled a long breath. "My brother isn't capable of a real apology."

"Sorry for bringing it up. You should probably pretend you're still crazy about me before everyone thinks we're fighting."

She grinned when I pulled her close, and I enjoyed the excuse to put my hands on her. "Just do me a favor and stay away from him."

"You know, fake or not, I'd never do that to you, don't you? Ever."

My gaze didn't leave hers. She couldn't know how much I appreciated her absolute promise. "Thank you." I couldn't stop myself from then suggesting, "You should probably kiss me. Lots of people looking."

She didn't disappoint, laying her hand against my chest and taking my lips without hesitation. Jesus. When she pulled away, I was hard pressed to let her.

"Sorry about your lip gloss. You'll probably have to reapply it."

"Any kiss worth having should mean I have to reapply my lip gloss."

She took my offered arm and walked with me into the hotel lobby. "I want to say one more thing about Chance, and then I'll drop it."

"What is it?" I asked.

"Remember that any reaction you have to him will make it seem as though you're still hung up on your ex."

I weighed her words. "I'm not hung up on her, you know." I wasn't sure who I was trying to convince, me or her, but I needed a change of subject. "Phil was talking about getting dinner next door after this. You up for it?"

"Of course. That's what I'm here for, to be your date."

"After being around this crowd, I wouldn't blame you if you're ready to call it a night."

"I'm okay. How do you feel after seeing the ex?"

"Fine. She wants to talk tonight, but it's just a closure thing."

Her body stiffened almost like she was jealous, but I was sure I had to be reading her wrong.

"Are you upset?"

She pasted on a smile. "No, of course not. You should do what you want. But do me a favor?"

"Sure."

"Don't make a fool of me. I may be here as your fake girlfriend, but that doesn't mean I don't have some pride invested here. If you want to get back with your ex, please don't do it until after the wedding."

I was already shaking my head, adamant that wasn't ever happening. "I'm not—" But we were already getting interrupted by Phil and Ellen.

"Hi, you guys planning on dinner?" Phil asked.

"We were just discussing. Teagan, this is Phil, and I take it you already met Ellen. And this is my girlfriend, Teagan." It was starting to get easier to roll off the tongue.

Phil and Ellen were good people, both of them now living in the DC area where they taught at a local university.

Two hours later, after enjoying dinner, we moved the party to one of the hotel bars. Thankfully, the bride and Vanessa had plans that didn't bring them to either of the locations we'd chosen. That meant I was less on edge and could actually enjoy myself. And more importantly, Teagan seemed to be having fun. It was great to see her in her element, her face flushed from a couple drinks, unregretful about ordering the pasta dish, laughing, and holding her own. I admired the way she was always true to herself. No pretense. No bullshit. Not for the first time, I realized how easy it was to be with her. Hell, Phil had even whispered to me earlier how much more relaxed I seemed to be. Sadly, he was right. Why hadn't I seen it sooner? I'd been under immense stress while with my ex. I could never do anything to her liking, no matter how hard I tried.

I pulled my phone out when it buzzed and immediately sighed at the notification. It figured. First chance in years I'd truly enjoyed a night out with my friends, and Vanessa would find a way to ruin it, sending me a text reminder she wanted to meet.

"Your nuts warm?" Teagan whispered with a grin.

I tried to return her smile. "They are. But are you ready to call it a night?" I took the last sip of my beer.

Phil downed the last of his drink too. "We should call it a night too. Golf is early tomorrow. We need to leave by seven for an eight a.m. tee time."

We both went our separate ways to opposite towers of the hotel.

Although Teagan and I were in the elevator alone, I enjoyed the way she kept hold of my hand. "Did you have a good time?"

Her smile was genuine. "I did. I worried earlier you might be surrounded by assholes, but Phil and Ellen are awesome."

"There's still plenty of assholes, but thankfully Phil and Ellen are the exception." We walked toward our room, and I slipped the key card into the door to let her precede me inside. Dammit, why did I feel guilty for what I was about to say? I hesitated at the door.

Turning to face me, she beat me to it. "It's okay. Go. I know it was Vanessa texting you at the restaurant."

Shit. Although Teagan was my fake girlfriend, I experienced very real guilt. "I won't be long."

She waved me off. "Take as long as you need."

"Will you wait up?"

She cocked her head to the side as if surprised by the question. Guess I was too, but I supposed I needed her to know I had every intention of coming back to the room.

"Guess it depends how late you'll be."

"I won't be long."

Vanessa was waiting for me downstairs in the lobby on one of the sofas. She stood as soon as she saw me approach.

"It's ridiculous to meet down here when I have an entire suite to myself where we could talk in private."

Had her voice always reminded me of nails on a chalkboard? I remembered a time when I'd sought to soothe her complaints, but now I found myself annoyed by them. "I'm not going up to your room. And I have only a few minutes."

"Why? Because you want to return to your new girlfriend? I hope you know she insulted the bride and your mother tonight. Is she the type of woman you want to be with?"

"She stood up for herself when both of them decided to go out of their way to insult her. Now please say what you need to say."

She sat down and scanned the lobby as I took a seat across from her. This was as private as it would get.

"I needed you to know your brother set me up."

I'd heard this excuse before, but honestly, I hadn't been calm enough to absorb the details. "How, exactly, did he do that?"

She looked excited I'd asked. "He made me think he wanted to be with me, but then staged the timing so you would interrupt us. But I never actually went through with it."

"Because I walked in on you both, not because you didn't want to."

"I was anxious and stupid, and I had cold feet or something about getting married. But I don't any longer. Now I know without a doubt how much I want to be with you. How much I want to be your wife. You've proven your point by bringing your little date with you. Congratulations, I'm jealous. It's what you wanted, right?"

To some degree, there was a small part of me petty

enough to admit it was. But a larger part of me found no satisfaction in her jealousy. "Vanessa—"

"I still love you, Reid. You've always been my forever. Since we were in middle school when you gave me a white flower and told me you thought I was beautiful."

The flower had actually been pink. Not sure why that tidbit stuck out now, but it did.

"We have so many years invested in each other. No one knows me better than you do."

This was probably true, but had she taken the time to truly get to know me? Or better yet, accept me for who I was? A flash of Teagan and me playing Mario Kart on my couch came up in my head.

"Vanessa, I—"

"No, don't say anything. Just think about it. Know I'll be here, waiting for you."

"I need to go." I was caught between frustration and anger, which meant I was better off keeping quiet. We had a wedding to get through, so upsetting Vanessa with harsh words would not make the rest of the weekend go smoothly.

"Okay. We'll plan to talk again soon?" She stood up and leaned in for a kiss but settled for my cheek when I turned my head.

My steps couldn't take me away fast enough. But I was so focused on getting back up to the room to Teagan, I walked straight into the one person I had no desire to talk to.

Chance.

He merely lifted a brow as he looked beyond me to where Vanessa stood. "Your new girlfriend aware you're down here talking with the ex?"

I loathed his smugness.

"Fuck off." I turned to go, not intending to say more than the two words to him. The simple sound of his voice triggered the feeling of betrayal all over again. I took one step before he spoke.

"Wait."

I didn't stop until his next word.

"Please."

I halted, but I didn't bother to turn around. "What do you want?"

His heavy sigh permeated the air. "To see you happy. Which begs the question of how well you know your new girlfriend."

I turned around, anger lacing every word. "You stay the hell out of my business and leave Teagan alone. You don't know the first thing about her."

"I know Mother can't stand her, the bride stares daggers at her, your ex is green with jealousy, and she basically told me to fuck off, so clearly Teagan has more going for her than anyone else you've dated."

My eyes narrowed at the unexpected compliment. "Exactly. So leave her alone."

"What did the ex want?"

"To get back together. To tell me how you set her up. It isn't happening." I'm not sure why I chose to share the words with him, but there was no mistaking the way his shoulders relaxed.

"Glad to hear it. You speak with Aiden lately? Have you heard how he's doing in Iraq?"

Since Aiden was a childhood friend of both of ours, it seemed petty to withhold information about him. "He should be back in the States this weekend."

"And the girl? What was her name—Chloe?"

I wasn't shocked to hear he knew about Aiden's girl. "He's moving to LA to be with her. It's a secret, though, so don't go and ruin anything."

He held up his hands in mock surrender. "I wouldn't dream of it."

"I need to go."

He gave me a curt nod. "You look good, brother. Happier than I expected to see you."

My molars ground together. "Must be the tropical air."

He shrugged. "Or the redhead. Good night."

Chapter Twenty-Four
TEAGAN

*I*nstead of spending my time pacing the floors while waiting for Reid to return from meeting Vanessa, I forced myself to get ready for bed. But now, instead of pacing, I was lying there feeling completely unsettled.

Dammit, fake girlfriend fail number thirty-seven if I was letting myself get upset that he was talking with his ex. I should know better than to let that bother me. Despite the intimate kisses and inside jokes, I'd never be more than his friend.

Stupid, stupid, stupid.

I needed to remember my place in all of this and not get wrapped up in the story.

How long had he been gone? Ugh. What if he'd met her in her room and they were— Nope, I wasn't going there.

The sound of the key card followed by the opening of the door had me sitting up. His footsteps were quiet as he walked into the bedroom.

"Hi," he whispered. "I didn't mean to wake you."

"You didn't. How did it go?"

He expelled a long breath. "Which part? Talking with my ex or talking with my brother?"

"Yikes. Please tell me they didn't meet you together?"

"No, no. I met Vanessa in the lobby and ran into Chance on the way back to the room. Then because I needed to cool down, I took a walk outside before coming up."

I hoped the conversations had been shorter than the walk. I could hear him slipping off his shoes before the distinctive swoosh of clothing. No big deal. Reid was just undressing for bed. The bed we were about to share.

"Hold on. Give me a few minutes to brush my teeth."

I waited, listening to the sound of the water in the bathroom and trying not to let the intimacy of the moment mess with my head.

"Are you sure you're okay with me sharing the bed? My offer stands to take the couch."

"It's a king size, so plenty of room. Sharing will be fine."

I tried to calm myself when the bed dipped, and then he was turned on his side, facing me, the moonlight illuminating his face.

"What did you say to my brother earlier?" he asked.

I repeated our conversation though I didn't know how he'd take it.

His laughter filled the room, causing me to feel immediate relief he wasn't upset by my unfiltered words.

"I'm sure Chance isn't used to having someone put him in his place."

"I'm surprised. He seems like enough of an asshole to warrant plenty of pissed-off people giving him a comeback or two."

He chuckled. "True, but when you're rich and the owner

of a lot of restaurants and clubs, I suppose you get away with a lot more."

"What kind of clubs?"

"Nightclubs, strip clubs, and who knows what else?"

"Your brother owns strip clubs?" My voice sounded high, even to my own ears. Although my moonlighting job in Dubai was completely secret, I didn't like the coincidence of the connection.

"Yeah, I forget how many, but most of them are in the LA area."

What a relief. "Have you ever been to one?" Color me curious.

"No. Definitely not interested."

His words were laced with disgust. If I'd ever had any doubt how he'd feel about me stripping, it was now obvious. "So let's rewind to your ex. What did she want?"

"She told me she'd been set up. That she didn't actually perform the deed."

"You think your brother set it up?"

"No doubt about it. He basically admitted he did it to save me. But it doesn't change the fact she wanted to."

I was quiet, absorbing his words.

"Can I tell you something I haven't ever said to anyone before?" he asked.

"Of course."

"I don't remember the last time I was truly happy with Vanessa."

Holy. Shit. It wasn't a declaration he was no longer in love with her, but it was a start. "What makes you say that?"

"Hindsight, I guess. I'm seeing her in a different light now. Anyhow, she did the usual: 'I want you back, I'm jealous, you proved your point by bringing a date, I'll wait for you, we have so many years invested.'"

Acid crawled up my throat. "What did you say in return?"

"Not much. I just wanted to leave."

Disappointment washed over me. So he hadn't told her he was done. He hadn't told her he no longer loved her. He hadn't slammed the door in her face. "Then you ran into Chance?"

"Yes, unfortunately. It pisses me off that he feels he's saved me. I won't give him the satisfaction of agreeing."

"Sounds to me like you could be tempted to get back together with Vanessa just in order to spite your brother."

"What? No."

"If she didn't make you happy and she was the type to cheat on you, I would hope you would've eventually realized it on your own."

He was quiet for a full minute, making me wonder what he was thinking.

"The thing is I don't know if I would have. I was blinded by this concept of investment. My thinking was I couldn't quit now when I had so many years invested. When I moved to Dubai, it was the first time I'd initiated the breakup. Every other separation had been her choice."

"How did breaking up with her feel?"

"Frankly, it was empowering. I'd finally made a choice for myself."

"Because she'd always held the power in the relationship?"

"Basically. It was on her terms more often than not. Yet the moment she flew to Dubai and promised she'd come live there with me, I took her back."

"Do you think you're angrier over the way things came to an end rather than the fact they ended? Maybe you're not ready to move on because it would mean you have to let go of your anger toward your brother. Almost like, on some level, you can't admit your brother cheating with your fiancée could turn out to be a good thing."

"I never thought of it that way."

We were both silent for a couple minutes. Then he killed any romance I could have been wishing for in one sentence.

"It means a lot to have a friend here with me to talk to about this stuff. Thank you."

"You're welcome."

He turned over, facing away from me. "Good night."

"Good night."

I WAS WARM. Too warm for some reason, but it took a moment, as my mind floated between sleep and consciousness, to recognize why. Suddenly, my eyes flew open at a decidedly foreign sensation.

Reid was wrapped around me, my back to his chest, as we both lay on our sides.

My heart wildly thumped against my chest as I enjoyed how good it felt to be wrapped in his embrace. As much as I didn't want to ruin the moment, I was quickly becoming aroused by the position. I shifted slightly, trying to put a little space between us, but his arm only tightened around me, pulling me closer.

The intimate contact robbed me of breath, especially once I felt the distinct bulge against my ass. Holy erection. Was it getting bigger. Yep. No mistaking it. My God, was he really that big? Just as I was contemplating how large he was, I was robbed of his heat when he suddenly pushed away.

"Shit. Sorry about the, uh, inadvertent snuggle," he muttered.

"It's okay." I turned over to face him.

He was on his back, an arm flung over his face. Could I help it if my eyes traveled south to investigate the mystery of Reid's size? Unfortunately, the comforter impeded any further investigation. Stupid cock-block comforter.

He reached for his charging cell phone on the nightstand, checking the display before resuming his previous position.

"What time is it?"

"Little after six."

"You have golf this morning?"

"Yeah, unfortunately."

"You don't enjoy golf?"

"Not my favorite activity, especially early in the morning."

"Trade you. You go to the spa with the catty women, and I'll go golf." I was less than thrilled to have a spa day on the agenda.

He moved to his side to face me, his grin making my stomach clench. Jesus. Reid Maxwell in the morning with the slight stubble was about the sexiest thing I'd ever seen. In contrast, I was sure my hair was a mess, and my breath smelled, well, like horrible morning breath.

"You're welcome to skip it."

"Really?" As much as a facial sounded divine, it wasn't worth the trouble of hanging out with the women.

"Absolutely. Do what you want for the day. We have the rehearsal and dinner tonight, but afterward we can go out just the two of us."

"Sounds good." After having him to myself the last few days, it was difficult to share.

"It will be nice to have the evening alone with you."

I tried not to read anything into his words. "I'll ask the concierge about places we could go. You getting out of bed?"

"Uh, yeah, but I'll probably wait a minute or two."

I couldn't help the grin spreading across my face. "Why is that?"

His entire face turned red. "You can guess why."

"Sorry, don't mean to make it hard on you."

He barked out a laugh. "Thanks for the assist. You giving me a hard time about my hard time has effectively deescalated the situation."

My laughter came easily although I felt a little guilty it was at his expense. Once he hopped out of the bed, I had to pretend I didn't want to stare at his ass encased in black boxer briefs. Jesus, I'd always known Reid was in decent shape, but my senses were overwhelmed by the sight of his back and shoulder muscles set off by his trim waist.

The sound of the water from the shower had me picturing him standing gloriously naked under the warm spray. Would he be jerking off? Had he been remotely tempted to take our morning position a step further? Ugh.

What I needed was an orgasm. And once he left, I'd have plenty of time to take care of things. Thank goodness I'd thought to bring my trusty vibrator along for the trip. I must have known I'd find myself sexually frustrated and in need of a good release.

A few minutes later, the water turned off. When Reid came out of the steamy bathroom, I nearly groaned aloud. He was wearing nothing but his khaki shorts, completely oblivious regarding the way his naked man chest affected me. Had I suggested he hit the gym? Seemed silly now. He was obviously already in terrific shape.

There was something weirdly personal in watching him go through his morning routine of shrugging into a shirt, threading his belt through the loops, and finally sitting on the bed to put on his socks and shoes.

"What will you do today?"

"Mm, sleep in." After an orgasm. "Maybe hit the gym, then the sauna." And have another orgasm. "Then I may sit poolside with an ice-cold cocktail to keep me company." Ellen had given me her cell phone number, so I might see if she could join me.

He flashed me a grin. The type which had me thinking I might need three orgasms to take the edge off.

"I'm jealous of your day. I don't know how late golf will go, but I'll text you from the road once we're on our way back."

"Take your time and have fun with your friends."

He stood up. "I forgot how nice it is not to have the pressure of dating."

Yep. Wouldn't want that, now, would we?

Once I heard the click of the door closing, I lay back in the bed with a gigantic huff. Yep, I'd been friend-zoned. Again. He'd said how nice it was not to be dating. Yet even if we were dating, I wouldn't have changed my words. I wanted him to have fun with his friends.

Dammit. I was doing it again. Spinning this fake relationship in my head.

Deciding now was a good time to chase away my unrequited feelings, I jumped out of bed and retrieved the little black satin bag from the zip pocket of my suitcase. I'd charged it before leaving, so it should be ready to go. Taking out the silicone hand-held device, I laid it on the bed while I shimmied out of my sleep shorts and thong. Settling myself on the comfy mattress, I turned the device all the way up to the highest.

What could I say? I wasn't a patient girl. And as for all the fancy settings? What was the point? Did anyone ever climax to the Morse code setting? Doubtful.

I preferred a straight vibration, so it could happen hard

and fast. As I lined up the working end of the small device to my clit, I thought of Reid this morning. Turning to my side, I imagined him behind me now, pushing into me while I used the toy. Would he be turned on by the thought of me masturbating while picturing him—or horrified? Oh, God. The vision of him pumping into me made my legs start to shake and my hips want to move. If only I had the real thing, but no matter. I was on the edge now, pressing the device into me to maximize the vibration.

I was so caught up in my need for the impending orgasm I barely registered the electronic sound of the door opening.

"Sorry, I forgot my wallet—" came Reid's voice.

I grasped for the bedspread, pulling it up to cover my naked half as I saw him frozen, one step into the bedroom, his face rapidly turning red.

"Shit—I didn't mean—"

"Sorry—I didn't know—"

Our frantic words bounced around the room until there wasn't a sound—except the buzzing.

Shit.

My fingers fumbled blindly to find the switch, only to hit the one that changed the pattern to rapid pulses. Fuck. Finally, I found the button to turn it off.

But still, he hadn't moved. Hadn't said another word.

I decided to break the silence in the hope it would also halt the eternal awkwardness and my humiliation, which seemed to be heating up my entire face.

"You forgot your wallet?"

"Uh-huh." He finally went into motion, stepping toward the dresser and grabbing his black leather wallet. "I'm so sorry."

"It's fine." It wasn't, but I'd wait until after he left to die of embarrassment. "It's just that after this morning in bed with you curled up to me—" Oh, sweet baby Jesus, what was I telling him?

Abort, abort, abort.

"I meant, it's fine. I don't want this to be awkward later."

Chapter Twenty-Five
REID

The thought of Teagan half naked under that comforter, her vibrator in her hand, had me frozen to the spot in shock.

Shock rendered me unable to move or speak at first, but once I realized I was only making the awkward situation worse, I grabbed my wallet. After that, I became intent on getting the hell out of here as quickly as possible.

Bang. Bang. Bang. The knock on the door was followed by Phil's voice.

"Reid, we're waiting on you. Kiss your girlfriend goodbye and let's go."

"I, um, again, I'm sorry." She appeared absolutely humiliated, and yet here I was, stammering like an idiot. Jesus, get it together and leave instead of staring like a pervert. "Bye."

Phil was waiting outside of the door with a knowing smirk. "I'm jealous of the reason that took you so long, but come on. Everyone is waiting."

It wasn't until I was seated on the bus that I replayed Teagan's words in my head. What did she mean after this morning in bed when I'd been curled up next to her? Had she been as turned on as I'd been after our accidental morning snuggle? My pulse leaped at the thought she'd wanted to touch herself because she'd been turned on by me.

This thought combined with the psychic's revelation Teagan might be too shy to make the first move, and suddenly I was anxious to return to her to see if this attraction was mutual. Too bad I was stuck with the group and reliant on the shuttle bus for the day. Otherwise, I'd have been tempted to try returning to the hotel. Then again, I needed some time to figure out what I was going to say. Would I ask her directly or wait to see how she reacted upon seeing me again? I only had a few hours, so I'd best figure it out.

I spent the day playing a mediocre game of golf while drinking beer with the guys. I'd never been one for either of those activities. However, it was better than having to attend a bachelor party at a strip club, so I had to count my blessings. Needless to say, I spent the whole time wondering what Teagan was doing.

After golf, we took the bus to a local bar for a few more rounds and some much-needed air-conditioning since we'd been out in the tropical sun all day. I still hadn't come up with an idea of what to say to Teagan once I returned. I texted her that we would be running late, and she'd replied that she and Ellen were at the bar having a drink before the rehearsal. I loved the way she made it so easy. No guilt trip. No reprimand. Just the message to take my time and have fun. Then again, perhaps she wasn't ready to see me yet. Perhaps she was humiliated about this morning. There was only one way to find out.

Unfortunately Teagan seemed to be the only one cool with us guys stopping for drinks. When our bus pulled up to the entrance of the hotel, the bride was standing there along with her mother and a few of her bridesmaids. Every one of them looked pissed off.

"We have the rehearsal in less than an hour, and all of you, you're drunk," Jamie screamed at the groom. Meanwhile, Vanessa glared at me as if I'd had something to do with the groom's choices. But instead of feeling like I had any hell to pay, for once I got to be the guy who waltzed on by without a care in the world.

"Reid, Reid," the voice from the past called out the moment I hit the lobby.

I forced myself to stop for Vanessa, who was approaching with quick steps in her high heels. She was completely decked out from head to toe, without a blond hair out of place or a smudge in her perfectly applied makeup, and yet I didn't so much as get a tingle. Instead, I was thinking about freckles, red hair, and a sharp wit.

"What is it?" My tone was curt.

She huffed, confusion splayed on her face, probably because I'd never spoken to her this way. Of course, I'd also never been more ready to dismiss her than I was in this moment.

"We can't be friendly now?"

I shook my head. "No. I'm realizing we never really were friends."

Her brown eyes filled with tears. Although it wasn't my favorite thing to see anyone cry, her tears no longer gave her power over me.

"I was hoping you'd had time to consider my words last night."

I hadn't needed to think about it. Not at all. "Yes, and I should've said it then, but we aren't getting back together. Ever."

Her eyes got big. "But I said I was sorry."

"And you know what? I forgive you." Namely because I no longer cared about her enough to hold a grudge. "You weren't happy. Hell, neither was I. And as much as I hate the way things happened, I'm beginning to realize it was for the best."

"You can't truly mean that."

I pulled away from her outstretched hand which was trying to take mine. "I really do mean it. Now, if you'll excuse me, I'm already late."

"It's her, isn't it? How long have you two been together? Were you cheating on me with a side piece in Dubai while I was getting ready to move there?"

My patience started to run thin. "You never had any intention of moving there, and I've never cheated on you."

Her chin lifted. "I don't believe you."

I wouldn't stand here one more moment while she twisted things. "Believe what you want. Frankly, I just don't care any longer. Now, if you'll excuse me."

I didn't wait for a reply, turning on my heel and walking to the elevators as fast as I could. I had one purpose now. Find Teagan.

I needed to see if this thing between us could possibly be mutual. For once, I wasn't worried I might still be hung up on my ex and how that might play out with a new romance. Instead, I was thinking of a fresh start. A new beginning with Teagan. Of course, there was the chance she didn't feel the same, but there was only one way to find out. I'd find her and see where her head was at about this morning.

After a quick shower, I dressed quickly in black trousers and a crisp gray shirt with a tie. I slipped on my loafers and bounded down the stairs with renewed energy. Time to find out how my fake girlfriend really felt.

I entered the lobby of the hotel and walked over to the

large promenade where most of the wedding party was gathered for the rehearsal. My eyes scanned the place for a few seconds before falling on Teagan standing outside on a nearby balcony. She was so beautiful with her red hair up, and her cobalt-blue dress clinging to the curves of her incredible body. Then, as if she could sense my gaze, she turned and gave me the type of smile that hit me straight in the gut.

My steps ate up the distance between us. "Hi." Jesus, was I sweating from a simple greeting? But I realized it was now or never. I'd make the first move and hope I wasn't reading the situation incorrectly.

"Hi," she greeted. "How was golf?"

"Good, but I was distracted all day. Can you guess why?"

Her entire face turned pink. "Was it what happened this morning?"

I leaned in, skimming the shell of her ear with my lips, enjoying the way she shivered at the light contact. "Yes. It's all I could think about all day. Now tell me. How many times did you come?"

Chapter Twenty-Six
TEAGAN

What the hell was happening? Had Reid just asked me how many times I'd come? My eyes were as wide as saucers, my face heated. Was he drunk? Was he joking?

Let's go with honesty for two hundred. "I didn't finish."

He leaned in again, the heat of his body seeping into mine with the contact. "What a shame."

Holy fuck. I was about to hyperventilate. But first, I was about to kiss Reid. For real, it seemed. Knowing this was our first real kiss was doing something to me. Heightening my senses, making my entire body shake with desire. When he pulled away, I felt dizzy. Drunk on whatever fantasy this was and hoping like hell it didn't stop.

My trance was abruptly ruined, however, once I looked over his shoulder, and spotted Vanessa standing there, rage reflected in her expression.

Shit. Had he done this for a show? Was this once again about her? But what about his words? There was no way those had been a fake, right?

The groom-to-be walked by, shifting my attention. His

face was pinched, the bride seemingly in a rage beside him. Damn. If you weren't happy during your wedding weekend, was it bound to work out?

"Um, things okay with the groom?"

"Nope. I imagine he just got an earful for showing up late and drunk. We went to the bar after our golf outing, which did not make the bride happy judging by the way she greeted the bus by screaming at him. But the guy deserved a bachelor party."

Translation. They'd been drinking all day. It suddenly occurred to me Reid might have said what he had under the influence of alcohol. The idea doused my hopes in cold water, yet he wasn't slurring and didn't seem intoxicated.

My emotions were completely at war with my brain, which was actively overthinking everything.

Reid tucked a strand of hair behind my ear. "How are your nuts?"

Hell if I knew. "Good. Fine."

"All right, I've gotta go do the groomsman thing for this rehearsal. Hopefully, it won't take long. Then we can eat dinner, listen to the toasts, and get back up to the room to be alone."

Dammit, there it was again. Him acting like this was no longer fake.

He didn't seem to notice my internal panic before he joined the other groomsmen to find their places on the promenade overlooking the beach where the wedding ceremony would take place tomorrow.

Forty-five minutes later, he finally rejoined me. He appeared none too happy they'd paired him with Vanessa. But what had he expected when the bride was her cousin?

After the bride and groom were done with more pictures, we all filed into the main restaurant on the other side of the hotel. They had a private room toward the back reserved for the wedding party.

Reid took my hand in his as if it was the most natural thing in the world. It had been natural when we'd been faking it, but what about now? After his words? My heart was slamming in my chest. I was afraid to hope, because hope set you up for disappointment. All of this meant I needed a drink. But I also needed to be sober enough to remember which fork to use.

Everyone around me might think this was a typical dinner, but my anxiety over my table manners or lack thereof was causing my leg to bounce under the table.

But Reid put his palm on my bare thigh to halt the movement, the heat of it burning my skin.

At least he grabbed his water first, which made it easy to know which glass was mine. I downed my full glass in one go, the liquid doing nothing to quell my sudden thirst. Where was my vodka?

With the arrival of the salad, I did as Chloe suggested and took my cues from the people beside me. Right. It was the smallest fork on the outside. And what about the roll? Okay, tear off little pieces. Jesus, I felt like a paranoid chipmunk, stuffing bread into my face while trying not to make a fool of myself. Glancing around, I saw the rest of the party was having a good time while I alone was obsessing. Stupid.

Two drinks later, I'd let go of my initial paranoia over table manners and was happily biting into my shrimp scampi.

"Quick question," I whispered to Reid after noticing the repeated death glares from the bridal party at the other end of the table.

He leaned over, moving his knee so it touched mine. "What is it?"

"Did something more happen with Vanessa?"

"Why do you ask?"

"Because she's murdering me with her glares. Which is nothing new, but it's extra murdery tonight."

He chuckled. "Nice word. Let's just say I'm ready to move on."

Move on. Meaning what exactly? I wanted to ask, but I was interrupted by the sound of a glass clinking. Evidently, it was time for the toasts, so I'd have to ask him later.

The remainder of the rehearsal dinner went by exceedingly slowly. I blamed Reid's touch. His palm on my leg, his knee against mine, or his hand holding mine under the table. Since none of them were outwardly affectionate gestures for anyone to see, I was confused as to the meaning of it all.

"Excuse me, I'm off to the ladies' room." I made my way to the rear of the spacious Mediterranean restaurant. As I walked into the restroom, I almost laughed out loud at how large it was. In addition to the regular bathroom with floor-to-ceiling stalls and opulent sinks with colorful tiles, there was also a side lounge room with overstuffed sofas. You knew it was fancy when you found a living room in a bathroom. The cotton towels placed by the sink only solidified the impression. This was definitely not a hand dryer kind of joint.

I had to fight the urge to snap a picture and send it to my sister.

After doing my business quickly, I came out of the stall to wash my hands and found Vanessa lying in wait. Frankly, I'd expected the confrontation sooner than this, so I shouldn't have felt surprised.

She didn't speak until I turned off the water and dried my hands, all the while effectively ignoring her presence.

"I hope you know Reid always comes back to me. Always."

I gave her a half shrug. "If that's the case, then there's no need to tell me."

Her beautiful face morphed into a snarl. Huh. Snarling Barbie was not a flattering look.

I took some lip gloss out of my purse and applied it with leisurely strokes, aware the action would demonstrate my indifference to her words. It was a calculated ploy I'd practiced over the years. Never let them see you sweat.

"You're nothing to him. Just a piece of trash he picked up on the side of the road to try to make me jealous for the weekend."

"Seems to be working." My eyes met hers in the mirror and registered the direct shot. If humans could froth at the mouth, I had no doubt she would be doing so now. Frothing Barbie.

"No one wants you here."

I finally turned around to lean against the granite countertop, popping the cap back on my lip gloss as though I found it more interesting than the conversation. "The man whose bed I sleep in does, and his opinion is all that matters to me."

I pushed off the edge, intending to walk around her.

But she moved in front of me, crossing her arms across her fake boobs.

This time I didn't bother to school my voice, letting it reflect my warning. "Move out of the way before I remove you. And believe me when I say you will regret the choice."

"Only because you're like an Amazon woman."

Lame. I'd hoped for something more cutting and creative.

"Middle school called. They want your insult back. By the way, you have red lipstick on your teeth." I made a motion with my finger toward my front tooth. "Whew, I've wanted to tell you all night as I could see it from all the way across the room. You're welcome."

"He'll come back to me. He always does," were her parting words as I moved past her and let the bathroom door cut them off.

Knowing history had yet to prove her wrong soured my victorious mood.

I pasted on a smile when I returned to the table, but Reid must've noticed something was off.

"What's wrong with the nuts?"

His mixed question combining our code words and what we were trying to avoid dragged a smile from my lips. "Nothing. Nuts are fine."

Ellen glanced from me to Vanessa, who'd also returned to the table, taking her seat near the bride. "I take it you had a little restroom confrontation?"

I took a sip of my martini. "Nothing I couldn't handle."

Reid arched a brow. "Of that I have no doubt."

After dinner, there were more freaking photographs to be taken of the bridal party. Deciding I wouldn't spend another minute watching Vanessa gloat as she stood next to Reid, I walked over to the adjacent terrace overlooking the ocean. Although it was dark, the full moon was bright. There was something soothing about the sound of the ocean waves and the warm breeze blowing at the outline of palm trees looming over the beach.

But I wasn't alone. The sweet smell of cigar hit my nostrils.

"If I didn't know any better, I'd think you're a stalker," I said recognizing the shadow.

Chance walked over and stood a few feet away to my left side. "I was out here first, so perhaps it's you who is doing the stalking."

"Don't flatter yourself."

"I'm surprised my brother didn't tell you to stay away from me."

He had, but I wouldn't give his brother the satisfaction of knowing it. "He doesn't need to. It's not as though I feel the urge to hang out with you."

"Yet here we are." He moved forward toward the railing to take in the view. "You know what I can't quite figure out?"

I schooled my tone to sound bored. "How to have a normal brotherly relationship? How not to be a dick? That's just a start, but I have other items on the list if you're searching for suggestions."

He chuckled, seemingly amused. "Perhaps, but the one thing on my mind is how much Reid is paying you to be here with him."

My fist clenched involuntarily at his audacity. I hated giving him the satisfaction of having even that small effect on me. "You know what I can't figure out? Why you despise your younger brother. Did he take your favorite toy growing up? Get all of Daddy's attention? Or is it just that while you're an asshole, your brother is actually a decent human being?"

He turned toward me, confusion splashed across his face. "I don't despise Reid. Not even in the slightest. But my job as his big brother is to protect him. Even from himself. If you have an agenda, I will find it out, Teagan, mark my words."

His cold promise sent a shiver of fear snaking through my body. The worst-case scenario would be for Reid to find out about my stripping. But the odds of anyone discovering my well-guarded secret were slim, especially since the job was in another country. "My agenda, unlike yours, is to see your brother happy."

He studied my face. "Interesting. You're in love with him."

I didn't bother to confirm or deny it. "As if you could recognize the emotion. Now if you'll excuse me, I have to get back."

Once pictures were over, I expected Reid might want to get cocktails in the lobby bar or hang out with his buddies, so I was surprised when instead he took my hand and led me to the elevator. "If you prefer to go out with your friends, I'd understand."

"I don't."

Once we reached our floor, he led me off the elevator and to our door. Nerves hit me. I felt as if the stakes had been raised, and the vibe was rapidly changing between us.

I preceded him into our room and turned with my mouth open to say something, but he caught me off guard, framing my face with his hands and crashing his lips down on mine.

Holy shit. He was kissing me. In the privacy of our own room without witnesses. When he pulled away, I found myself standing there like a deer in the headlights.

His eyes searched mine. "Is this okay?"

"Uh-huh," came my highly sophisticated answer as I dropped my purse to the floor and met his lips again. Oh, God. This was happening. Why the hell did I have to be so much inside of my head to question what I'd always wanted? But I couldn't help it. I had to ask.

"Wait, is this real? Are you drunk?"

He moved his kisses to my neck. "Definitely not drunk. Definitely not fake."

A part of me was tempted to ask if this was a reaction to the scene he'd witnessed this morning. As far as I knew, he'd been without sex for months. We'd been sharing fake kisses and a bed with inadvertent morning wood snuggles—and then he'd walked in on me masturbating—so it seemed plausible we'd find ourselves at this point.

But was it circumstance, or could it be more? More importantly, if I tried to define matters in the moment, would I ruin the natural flow of things? But if I went with the flow, I was taking a risk this would all blow up in my face. In the end, there was no way I could stop. I'd just have to deal with the consequences later.

My tongue tangled with his, and when he gently nipped my bottom lip, the sound of my groan filled the room. His fingers came up to tangle in my hair, pulling out the pins and letting it fall down around my shoulders.

Stepping back from him, I unzipped the side of my dress, all the while watching his eyes track my lowering hand. Could he see I'd started to shake? Could he tell how nervous I was? Once the zipper was down, I peeled off one shoulder and then the other, baring myself in nothing but my bra from the waist up. I didn't miss the way he inhaled an unsteady breath.

After moving the material down past my waist and over my hips, I let it fall to the floor, leaving myself standing there in nothing but my pink lace bra and matching thong.

"I thought you said pink wasn't your color." Reid's voice was thick, his gaze sliding down my entire body.

Leave it to him to remember. "It's not my color, but that doesn't mean I don't secretly like it."

He grinned, closing the distance and framing my face with his hands. "You're stunning."

"You're overdressed."

His chuckle filled the room. Then it was his turn to step back. He began with his tie and then unbuttoned the dress shirt. Jesus, I'd never experienced anything hotter than watching this man undress, his eyes not leaving mine.

The anticipation crackled through the air. I half expected the moment to be interrupted with a knock on the door or an urgent phone call. That would be my luck. But fortunately, nothing spoiled the moment.

Reid stopped stripping once he'd fisted his T-shirt over his head and lost his shoes, choosing to leave his trousers on—much to my disappointment.

I made to lose my high heels too, but he wasn't having it. "No, leave them. I want to fuck you with them on."

His command was hot. Not to mention unexpected. I would have expected polite Reid to ask if I minded. But polite Reid wasn't here. He'd been replaced by alpha Reid. And I loved every second of it. I didn't hesitate to move onto the bed, watching him remove his belt before he stalked toward me.

He leaned over me, grasping both ankles and pulling me to the edge of the bed and closer to him. I gasped when he knelt down and rubbed his hands along my thighs. His touch was warm, sensual, and unhurried. Once he'd slowly trailed his hands up to my hips, he hooked my thong with both thumbs and peeled it down the length of my legs, afterward tossing it onto the floor. His eyes burned into my skin as he looked up, lust evident on his face.

"Christ. You're perfection. Take off your bra. Let me get the full vision."

I undid the front clasp, letting the material fall away to the sides and grinning at his growl.

"Jesus. You're more than I ever could've imagined."

He widened my legs with the width of his shoulders as he dipped his head, landing kisses on my thighs, then above the place I desired him most.

"Do you have any idea how long I've waited to taste you?"

Wait. What? "How long?"

He blew a warm breath over my most intimate place, causing a shiver through my body. "Truth?"

"You're between my naked thighs and inches from my pussy. I don't believe a lie will do."

His sheepish grin made me giggle. "Since the first time we fake kissed in my apartment."

I sucked in a breath at the admission. "You're serious?"

He moved forward, running his tongue along my seam. Oh. My. God.

"Would this tongue lie to you?"

"Not if it's busy doing other things."

His chuckle was muffled once he dove into my center.

I gripped the sheets, trying to anchor myself for his welcome assault. I'd never been the type of girl to come quickly with oral, and yet here I was, already on edge, rocking my hips against his face, panting like I'd run a race.

"Please," I begged, needing the release more than my next breath.

Chapter Twenty-Seven
REID

I'd never been so turned on as I was in this moment. So absolutely fixated on one thing. The most stunning, funny, incredible woman who was currently muttering a string of curses while I feasted on her. I loved having her like this. Wild at my touch, writhing with pleasure, and unabashed in threading her fingers through my hair to pull me in closer.

She tasted incredible. Just as I'd imagined. Deciding to double down on my efforts, I focused on her clit and inserted a finger into her tight pussy. The sound of her groan made my cock strain against my trousers. She was so responsive. So wet. So fucking sexy.

Inserting another finger, I curled them up to reach her G-spot and knew the moment I'd found it by the way her hips flew off the bed.

"Oh, God, Reid. Oh, God," she chanted, her body seizing up before convulsing in a spectacular climax. I took the opportunity to lick her clean.

When I stood up, she lay back, her perfect chest heaving, one arm thrown over her face, her hair fanned out and wild on the sheets. She made an erotic picture. I crawled onto the bed with her, kissing up her flat stomach, marveling at how soft her skin was as my hands feathered over her sides and up to her breasts. Her incredibly round, naturally perfect breasts.

I could imagine many a naughty thing I'd love to do with them, including sliding my cock between them toward her plump lips. Later, though. Currently I was on borrowed time if I didn't seek to embarrass myself.

I stood up, watching her track my movements. The slide of my zipper, the clasp of my trousers, and then the pooling of the material when I pulled them down my legs, taking my socks with them.

Lastly, my boxer briefs hit the floor.

"Damn. I wasn't the only one with a secret beneath my clothes." Teagan sat up on the bed, her gaze focused on one thing.

Yeah, so I was blessed in the size department. Her unabashed perusal sent heat to my face.

"You secretly liking pink isn't quite the same as my dick size."

She grinned, rising up to her knees and scooting toward the edge of the bed where she could reach out and grab a hold of me. "You're right. The size of your cock is a much better surprise."

My eyes closed at the sensation of her hand wrapped around my shaft. But they flew open the moment she put her mouth on me. There was no hesitation. No tentative movements or working up to my size. No, instead she wrapped those glorious lips around the tip and slid down the length until she could take no more.

"Christ. Your mouth feels like heaven."

The hmm sound she made in response vibrated down into

my balls. Teagan was now caressing them with one hand while the other gripped my base to jerk me off in combo with her mouth. The sensation was the most incredible thing I'd ever experienced. But it also meant I was getting close. Too close.

"We'd better stop before I come."

She licked the crown like it was a lollypop and glanced up to meet my stare. "Why would I stop before you come?"

Proving her point, she intensified the cadence with her hand while snaking her tongue down the length of my shaft. When she got to my balls, her lips took no prisoners.

My legs shook uncontrollably while my muscles clenched. "I'm close."

Instead of easing off of me, she swallowed me deep, hollowing her cheeks and taking me to the back of her throat. My hand rested on her hair, trying not to apply too much pressure, but her garbled words stopped me altogether.

"What?" I asked.

She popped off. "I said, pull it like you want it."

I muttered a curse at the free license she was giving me. She had no idea the beast she was awakening. My fingers curled around in her hair, running through it and pulling it tight while she bobbed up and down.

It was so unbelievably hot, but once she reached down to rub her own clit, I was a goner. I threw my head back with a roar, my hips arching as I finished myself in her mouth. I looked down again to see her swallow it up as if it was her singular mission in life. She kissed me one last time on the tip before leaning back on her haunches with a satisfied grin.

I could picture nothing better than to sink deep inside of her, but there might be a problem. "Shit."

Teagan giggled. "Well, there's a reaction every girl hopes to hear after giving a blowjob."

My grin came easily. I cupped her chin, not hesitating to kiss her lips. "Sorry, I was thinking about condoms and if I had any. If not, then I'll have to get dressed and head in search of some in the shop downstairs." I scanned the floor for my trousers. Taking out my wallet, I prayed. "Aha. One lucky one."

She grinned. "It is lucky."

I laid it on the bedside table.

"Did you need me to help you put it on?"

"No, because first I have some making up to do." I climbed into the bed, settling her beside me.

"Making up?"

My hands skimmed down her side, my fingers splaying over her stomach as I marveled at the flawlessness of her luminous skin. "Mm, you have the most incredible body I've ever seen, and yet I hardly paid it enough attention. I intend to spend some time worshiping it now."

I dipped my head to take one of her hardened nipples into my mouth, using the other hand to cup and squeeze her other breast. "At some point I plan to slide my cock between these beauties and fuck your mouth."

Her eyes went wide. Oh, crap, was she offended by my frank talk? But then she rose up and took my lips in what could only be described as the most passionate kiss I'd ever received.

My tongue tangled with hers, wanting nothing more than to prolong this moment.

But she wasn't having it. "This may surprise you, but I'm not a very patient person."

My grin was back. Since when had sex been such an incredible combination of playful and sexy? It was everything I never knew I'd been missing.

"What are you impatient for?"

"I need you inside of me."

I'd have to take a rain check on exploring her body because my control was hanging by a thread. "Let me get the condom on."

It took me a few seconds to wrap up and position myself between her legs. I notched the head against her opening, sliding in slowly, letting her accommodate to my size. "You okay?"

"Yes. More, please."

Whew. Because holding still was torture. I pushed in deeper, paying attention to her face and the perfect O her lips were making at the sensation.

"You feel incredible."

"That mean I can push in further?"

"There's more?" she squeaked, making me grin and blush at the same time.

"I can stop here." It would be torture, but I'd do it.

"Hell no, give it to me. All of it."

Thank God. I pushed in slowly in case she was in pain, but I didn't see any signs of it. Just when I was about to check in with her, she wrapped her long legs around my waist to pull me into her. The sensation caused my mind to go blank. The feeling of her tight, wet pussy stripped away all other memories of sex before her.

When her hands slid up my back, and her nails dug in, I had to move.

"It's so good," she groaned, taking my lips in a punishing kiss.

I needed her to come again. To see the satisfaction on her face as she milked my cock. Putting my hands under her ass, I lifted her hips up and drove into her hard and deep. She held on, meeting my thrusts in perfect rhythm.

She was loud, aggressive, and incredibly responsive. It was as if she'd taken sex, and dialed it up to ten. Her inner muscles clamped down, and she came with spectacular force.

My climax closely followed, the power of which nearly took my breath away.

Chapter Twenty-Eight

TEAGAN

"Wow. That was unexpected."

We lay naked and entangled in the bed as our breathing finally returned to normal. I was in awe. Sex with Reid had been incredible.

"Should I be insulted you didn't expect it to be amazing?" Humor infused his words.

"No, I meant I had no clue you were interested in, you know, more than a friend and fake girlfriend." For all I knew, this had only been about sex, and yet every fiber of my being hoped it involved more than a convenient release.

He rolled to his side, so he could face me. "The tongue down your throat earlier didn't clue you in I might want more than friendship?"

"So your ex could witness it? No."

His forehead crinkled up. "What are you talking about?"

"The kiss. Vanessa was standing behind us, so I figured it was for her benefit. Although your whispered words were definitely not for her, so I was confused."

He shook his head. "I had no idea she was there. Hopefully, by now you realize this is real."

I decided to put a toe into the water to check the temperature of the relationship. "What is 'this,' exactly?"

"What do you want it to be?"

Shit. He'd turned my question around. "I don't— I mean, I'm not sure." I wasn't convinced he was completely over his ex. This could potentially be rebound sex for him. Or it could be something more. It wasn't as if I'd ever been in a relationship and knew what to expect.

"How long have you been thinking about something more physical?"

I decided to share a version of the truth. "Our first kiss was more than I was expecting too. But I thought you were unaffected."

His eyes went big. "I was the opposite of unaffected."

"You were af-fected?" I teased.

"To the point of second-guessing this entire idea. Because how do you fake it with someone you're actually attracted to?"

Blink. Blink. Blink. "Good question."

Tell him.

Shut up, stupid internal voice. You just had incredible sex, you do not need to go and tell him you've had a crush on him for the past year. You don't know what will happen after this weekend. You need to go with the flow.

I watched him get up to take care of the condom and immediately missed his heat.

"What, um, made you decide to take a chance?" I asked.

"After your slip this morning in saying you were turned on by our snuggle, I remembered the psychic's clue that you were too shy to make the first move. So I thought I'd take the chance you might feel the same as me."

"I'm glad you did."

He got back into the bed, gathering me close and kissing my lips. "Me too."

FINDING myself in Reid's arms in the morning was like a dream, one I didn't want to wake up from. I feared the AM would bring about some degree of regret on his part or a confirmation he'd been acting on the rebound.

So much for going with the flow. So much for being content to see this through one step at a time. Dammit, I was overanalyzing it.

"Mm, for a non-morning person you are awfully awake already."

I grinned into my pillow. "I was thinking this is déjà vu of yesterday morning."

He pushed against me. "Except we're quite naked, and I don't have to go take a shower to relieve myself in secret, and you won't have to play with your toy once I've left. By the way, I have plans tonight for you and your little toy."

I loved how hot he was in the bedroom. It was so unexpected. "You positive we need to attend the wedding today? I can concoct much better activities to keep us busy."

"Me too. At least we have a few hours before I need to be anywhere."

I gasped when his fingers came around to play with my clit, the hardness behind me making me wet with anticipation.

"Shit," he cursed when I moved so he could notch himself between my thighs.

"Keep saying that, and a girl is bound to get a complex."

He chuckled in my ear. "We used my one and only condom. I'll need to go find a shop that's open at this hour."

"Shit," I echoed, making us both crack up. "I suppose it's been awhile since you've had to use condoms?"

"I always used condoms. Vanessa had a thing about taking the pill, so I always wore them. Honestly, I don't think she enjoyed the idea of me coming inside of her."

I started coughing for the same reason I'd choked on my drink last night, prompting Reid to thwack me between my shoulders yet again this weekend.

"If I didn't know better, I'd say you have quite a problem with swallowing."

We faced one another now. "But you do know better."

"I do know." He pulled away. "Give me a few minutes to, um, deflate the situation so I can go downstairs. Unless you're on birth control and want to talk about going without?"

My eyes widened at the magnitude of the conversation. It was one I'd never had with a man. "I'm on the pill, and I have absolutely no opposition to you coming inside of me. You'd be the first."

His eyes went dark with desire. "I'm clean. To be safe, I got tested after Vanessa cheated. But I've never not used a condom, not with anyone."

"I'm clean too, so we're okay without a condom?"

His face heated. "If it's too soon—"

"It's not." He'd never gone without a condom, not even in his long-term relationship. But he wanted to go bare now, with me.

Gah, don't read into it. The best way to keep from more overthinking was to straddle the gorgeous man beside me. Judging from his expression, he was a fan.

"You going to do all the work?" he quipped, bringing up my joke from yesterday.

"Sure, baby, you just lie there and enjoy," I purred, wrapping my fingers around his cock and squeezing.

"Jesus, is it wrong to find that kind of hot?"

I giggled, loving his playful side in the bedroom. "No, but it does mean I'd miss out on you grabbing my ass as I ride you."

"Fuck," he muttered, his eyes widening as I rose up above him, notching the head of his cock against my opening.

But it was my turn to curse as I fed him inside of me and felt a twinge of pain from his size. Maybe this wasn't the best position given how large he was.

"Are you wet enough?" he asked, moving his fingers to my clit.

"Maybe not." I let out a shriek when he flipped me on my back and dove between my legs. "You can't do that— We had sex last night, and I haven't showered."

"As if I care," he murmured a split second before my clit went between his teeth. I whimpered when he plunged his fingers inside of me.

He teased me until I was practically clawing at the bed. His fingers moved in and out of my slick entrance while his talented mouth traveled south. I inhaled when his tongue speared into me while his thumb rubbed my clit with diabolical attention. "Come for me now."

The gentle demand was all it took. My body went taut, melting from the scorching wave of heat that rolled through me from head to toe. I came with an explosive cry.

My muscles were still spasming when he flipped us back into our previous position with me straddling him.

"Put me inside of you," he panted, holding my hips so I had leverage to impale myself on his shaft.

His eyes closed, and he heaved a hiss between his teeth.

"Too tight?"

"No. God, but the sensation is so fucking good to be inside of you bare."

My eyes met his, heightening the intensity of the moment. I placed my hands on his chest and sank down to take him to the root, reveling in the fullness for a moment before I rose up and began to ride him.

I controlled the rhythm at first, but soon he was thrusting up as I ground down. We were both chasing an orgasm, but it was me who got there first, detonating atop him. I felt his fingers grip me close as he thrust up one last time, holding me still as he emptied himself deep inside of me.

Jesus. I knew without a doubt I was ruined for any other man. But now wasn't the time to freak out about it.

There was a delicious soreness between my legs and a permanent smile on my face by the time we dressed for the wedding. Although I cringed at the amount of money Reid had spent on my dress, I had to admit the floral print wrap dress looked great. I twisted my hair up in a simple updo and put extra effort into my makeup.

As I fastened my earrings in the bedroom mirror, he came up behind me to drop a kiss on my bare shoulder. "You look beautiful. The Marc Jacobs was a good choice."

"Who?"

He chuckled. "The designer."

The fact he remembered when I did not should have been a reminder of our different worlds.

"I forgot how nice it is you don't care about stuff like that."

"Is it?" My question sounded casual, yet the meaning behind it wasn't as I could feel my insecurities threaten to take over.

He only smiled. "Of course. Now then, you ready to go downstairs, so we can get this evening over with and return to the room?"

I turned around to smooth my hands down the front of his tuxedo. "Seeing you in this tux makes me wish we could skip the wedding altogether."

He smiled. "Me too, but we'll cut the night short and be back up here in no time."

Twenty minutes later, pictures of the bridal party were underway. I didn't miss the way Vanessa stood closer to Reid than necessary, and touched him incessantly. When he murmured something to her, she laughed as if they'd shared a private joke. My stomach clenched, jealousy a tough emotion to tamp down. Too bad there wasn't a pre-wedding open bar. At least Ellen provided a great distraction.

"If you ever end up in the Washington, DC, area, Phil and I would love to see you again. Or, hey, Phil said Reid might be moving to Sydney. So maybe we'll make a trip down under to visit you two."

Her words reminded me that I probably wouldn't see them again in the future, and also how my days with Reid were numbered if he did take the job. "It would be great to have you visit." I meant the words even if they weren't going to come true. Reid and I hadn't talked about a future. Beyond tonight, there might not be one.

Chapter Twenty-Nine
REID

I couldn't remember being so happy. So content with how my future was shaping up. With Vanessa I'd always felt on edge and uneasy, if I was being honest with myself. It had been a constant roller coaster of emotions. But with Teagan, there was this connection I couldn't put into words.

But I didn't want to spook her. You didn't take someone to a wedding as your fake girlfriend and then turn around and tell her you were falling in love with her the same weekend. I hoped we could both return to Dubai and let things happen for real.

After a grueling wedding ceremony with the island sun beating down, we were finally indoors for the reception. The sooner this was over, the faster I could have Teagan naked beneath me. The sex was incredible. The connection, the playfulness, the heat. When it came to chemistry, it was off the charts. I craved her in a way I'd never before experienced.

"Penny for your thoughts," I whispered in Teagan's ear while we were on the dance floor. I was happy to be taking a break from wedding duties and holding her in my arms.

"Mm, my thoughts are not suitable for saying out loud."

Her words made me instantly hard, and because I wanted her to notice, I pulled her closer.

"Ooh, this dance just got interesting. Sadly, you may have to rein it in as I see the photographer trying to round up the wedding party."

I groaned, having already been through countless photos. "Great. More pictures of a couple who'll be lucky to make it to five years."

She leaned back, meeting my eyes with clear amusement. "Who's the cynical one now?"

"Perhaps I am. But then again, I've never heard two people on their wedding day sound so miserable together."

I could very well have ended up in the same boat. Although I doubted I'd ever reach a place where I was thanking my brother for helping me dodge a bullet, I was at least grateful to be where I was now: dancing with a beautiful woman with whom I could genuinely see a future. Teagan was someone who accepted me for who I was instead of requiring my bank account or family name. Someone who made me laugh, challenged me in all the right ways, and approached life without apology.

I could see the bridesmaids waving me over, including Vanessa, who seemed all too pleased to interrupt my dance.

"Sorry, gorgeous, duty calls." I dropped my hand to her ass and gave it a subtle skim.

Her grin was contagious. "Aw, you remembered. I knew you had it in you."

"Like you once said, it would be a shame not to appreciate such an impressive backside."

"It would indeed."

My lips dropped to hers for another kiss. "I hope I won't be long."

"I'll be bellied up to the bar if you want to find me afterward."

After a million more pictures, I was finally able to break away. Unfortunately, I didn't get far before my mom and Vanessa's parents intercepted me. I suppose I should have been thankful they hadn't converged on me earlier. "Hello, Mother and Mr. and Mrs. Lane. Nice to see you."

Mr. Lane shook my hand while Mrs. Lane gave me kisses on both cheeks. "Please call us Betsey and Steve," she said. "Or I was hoping for Mom and Dad."

Wasn't happening. "Beautiful wedding."

Betsey pursed her lips. "Under the unfortunate circumstances, I suppose it was." Leave it to her to take a swipe at her sister's daughter for the unplanned pregnancy. "So Vanessa tells me you two have talked. I have high hopes for a reconciliation."

Who knew what she'd told them, but I found I didn't care. "It was nice to see you both. If you'll excuse me."

I had thought to escape to the bar and find Teagan, but my mother was hot on my heels. "I cannot believe you'd embarrass me like that. I raised you better than that, Reid Matthew Maxwell."

I turned to face her. "Actually, Mona raised us while you were traveling the world with your boyfriends."

She didn't bother to defend herself. "You're throwing away your chances here on this—what? This little flavor of the month."

"Don't." My temper flared at her audacity.

"You don't understand what you're giving up. The Lanes have so much influence and—"

"You mistakenly presume I care about any of that superficial load of crap, illustrating how little you know me." My mother had always been hung up on old money and keeping up pretenses. I was so relieved to be away from all of it.

"You're like your father. Selfish."

"No, he's not," came Chance's voice from behind me. "If anyone is selfish, I'd say I get the unfortunate distinction."

My mother's glance bounced from me to him. She then huffed. "All the men in my life are selfish."

"The men in your life prefer to call it self-preservation," Chance quipped, earning a twitch of my lips since he wasn't wrong. I'd grown up privileged, but the only one who'd ever looked out for me was the guy doing so right now.

"Your new fling is absolutely not invited into my home for the holidays—if it even lasts that long."

"It will last, and there's a simple fix. I won't come home." The thought of skipping the holiday family events sent a rush of relief through me.

She gave one more glance between me and Chance and sighed heavily before turning on her heel, leaving me with my brother.

"You're serious about Teagan, I take it?"

My eyes narrowed. "It's none of your business. Leave her alone, Chance. I mean it." The sting might have dimmed regarding his betrayal with Vanessa, but that didn't mean I was ready to trust him.

He held up his hands as though he was surrendering the cause.

At the same time, my phone buzzed. It was a text from Aiden.

"Aiden is with Chloe in LA. They reconciled."

Chance appeared surprised I was sharing the news with him. What could I say? Some habits were hard to break.

"I appreciate you telling me."

"If you'll excuse me, I know Teagan will be anxious to hear the same news."

"Why's that?"

"Chloe is her best friend."

His brows contracted at the tidbit of information I'd shared. But it was a harmless detail. If he thought to get to Teagan by ferreting information from Chloe, he'd be out of luck.

Chapter Thirty
TEAGAN

I considered myself a brave person. However, approaching Reid while he was with Vanessa's parents and his mother was not happening under any circumstance. There was brave, and then there was reckless. A smart woman stayed at the bar.

"I'll take a bourbon neat and a gin and tonic, please," I told the bartender. Gin was a safe bet for keeping me on good behavior. The bourbon, of course, was for Reid because I knew he'd need it.

Turning around with the drinks in hand, I caught Reid stalking toward me with heated eyes. Jesus. If ever there was a look a man gave a woman to make her knees weak, this was it. He stared at me as if he saw no one else. It was both exhilarating and terrifying.

"I got you a drink."

He took the cold glass and used his free hand to take mine. "Thank you. Any chance you want to take off and return to the room now?"

"Are we allowed?" Dinner had been served, the cake had

been cut, and the toasts had been made. Dancing was still in full swing, but hell if I knew the protocol.

He chuckled. "I've done more than my duty. Come on."

I giggled. Actually giggled like a teenage girl as I followed him through the reception and into the lobby. Once we were in the elevator, he didn't hesitate in seizing the moment to take my lips.

Breathless.

How could a simple kiss leave me this way? But here I was, gazing into his eyes and swallowing hard at how far gone I was for this man. My stupid brain hoped for confirmation he was feeling it too, while my body argued against any sort of heavy conversation that might rob it of future orgasms.

I was team orgasm all the way.

Once we were in the room, we quickly stripped out of our clothes like it was a race, grinning the entire time. I stood naked in victory. "I win."

He glanced up from undoing his trousers, the last article left of his clothing. "Do you? I'd argue I'm the one winning since I get to stare at your body first. Why don't you get on your hands and knees up near the headboard, beautiful."

He didn't have to ask me twice. It was a position we hadn't tried yet, and I looked forward to him taking me from behind. But once the bed shifted under his weight, I expected him to come up behind me. Imagine my surprise when I felt a wet tongue instead.

I moaned, looking down to see him between my legs. Had I ever witnessed a sexier sight in my life?

"Lower yourself so you straddle my face."

My hands gripped the headboard for leverage as I lowered myself to his waiting lips. "Full disclosure. If you die, you die."

He chuckled. "I'll take my chances."

When his mouth fastened on my clit, I nearly bucked off of him.

"Ride my mouth."

So. Fucking. Hot.

I did as he asked, getting into a rhythm before he took hold of my hips and held me for an incredible assault of lips, tongue, and fingers.

"Oh, God." I threw my head back and death-gripped the headboard, hoping it was sturdy enough to sustain my climax. Holy shit. A moment of blackness overwhelmed my senses, causing everything to block out except for the waves of pleasure hitting my body over and over.

As I came down off my orgasm, I realized I'd gripped my thighs together as I'd lost my mind. "Jesus, sorry."

He chuckled, probably thankful I was letting him breathe again, and slid out from my thighs. "You did warn me."

"I did, but wow."

He wasn't done. Warm hands rubbed my back, then up to my shoulders. "Do you have any idea how sexy you are? I'm addicted to touching and tasting your soft skin."

Once again, the compliment landed, and I wasn't sure what to do with it. But this time I didn't refute it. Instead, I turned my head over my shoulder to meet his kiss, pouring all of my love for this man into the only way I dared show him.

Dammit, did I use the word love?

Yes, yes, I did. Was there really any doubt I was in love with him?

Great. Now I was having internal conversations with myself.

Shut up, self. Kiss this amazing man and stop questioning his motives.

"You tasting yourself on my lips has to be the hottest thing ever."

"Mm, I wouldn't ever miss a chance to kiss you."

He laid his hand on my face, searching my eyes. Holy intensity. Could he read my internal thoughts? Gulp. He had no idea how close I was to blurting out my feelings.

"Tell me what you're thinking."

"I really like you." Lamer words had never been uttered.

But he grinned. "Good, because I really like you too."

All talking ceased. He took my lips in a deep kiss, his tongue tangling with mine. We shifted ourselves so we were both lying on our sides, legs intertwined, bodies on fire. He leaned back, the heat blazing from his eyes as he tracked his gaze down my body.

"I need you inside of me. Now." I could hear an unfamiliar desperation in my voice.

"Get back on your knees."

He got behind me, parting my lips and rubbing the head of his cock along my wetness.

I bit down on my lip at the sensation of him slowly notching inside of me.

"Sore?"

"A little. But only in the best way possible."

He groaned when I pushed back, taking him in deeper while my pussy stretched to accommodate his size.

"Oh, my." A phrase I didn't think I'd ever spoken but was so very appropriate for the fullness I was experiencing. He was so unbelievably deep. My hands found purchase on the sheets as I started my rhythm of pushing back, and I gasped when he reached around to strum my clit.

"Rise up and reach back to give me your lips."

He assisted me by banding his arms around my waist and chest, holding me in position so I could arch my head back and meet his lips. Oh my God.

He took over the rhythm by digging his fingers into my

skin and thrusting deeper and deeper with every stroke. When his hand reached down to find my clit, I was done for. Searing heat snaked through me. I cried out while riding the waves of pleasure. He growled in my ear with a final thrust, grinding out his own orgasm deep inside of me.

We collapsed on the bed together where I enjoyed the way he held me there, my back halfway across his chest, our heartbeats erratic, our breathing in synch.

"I didn't believe it was possible, considering how good it was the first two times, but sex with you just keeps getting better."

I lifted my head to flash him a smile. I'd been thinking the same thing.

The sound of the phone buzzing interrupted the moment. It was coming from the floor where his trousers lay. "It's your phone."

"Mm, let it buzz." He lifted me up and to his side, tucking me in closely. "Oh, that reminds me. Aiden texted. He's in LA and surprised Chloe there."

"Yes, I know. She sent me a text too. She's so happy."

When his phone buzzed again, he cursed but made no move to get it. The knowledge he wasn't in any hurry to break this moment filled me with contentment.

"Aiden is happy too. Speaking of which, how would you feel about me traveling to LA with you tomorrow?"

Excited. Nervous. Freaking out. "Sure." God, I'd been hoping to act cool, but instead I'd overshot.

"I would get a hotel since I know you're staying with your sister. Don't worry. I thought perhaps I'd go see Aiden, and maybe we could go out with him and Chloe, but I'm not crashing your vacation. Promise."

I wanted him to come with me. Meet my sister. Meet my niece. But then he'd see the not-so-great apartment and neighborhood where I'd grown up. "Yeah. No. I want you to go."

He chuckled. "Yeah, no. You're very convincing."

Dammit, words. Why were you failing me? There was so much I wanted to say. Especially since this was an important step. A possible relationshippy step. But unfortunately, we were interrupted by another round of his phone buzzing.

"Let me check this real quick." He jumped out of bed while I lay there and admired his impressive backside.

"Ugh. It's my mother. She's called twice and is now texting to say she's leaving tonight and wants to apologize before she goes." He took a seat on the bed and scrubbed a hand over his face. "She doesn't often say she's sorry."

"Then you should go. I'll be right here keeping the bed warm." Frankly, I'd use the time to gather my thoughts and figure out how to tell him I was excited about the idea of him accompanying me to LA tomorrow. Maybe I could start by sharing some of my fears with him. Hopefully, he could give me some confidence about the direction we were heading.

"You certain you don't mind?" He started gathering his clothes from the floor.

"I don't although don't be surprised if you get roped into more pictures."

He cursed under his breath. "I'm leaving the jacket and tie in the room to ensure they won't grab me for more pics. How many does the bride need?"

"I have no clue. I swear by all that's holy that when I get married I will not be burdening my bridal party with three photographers and a drone."

"Good to know." He winked before disappearing into the bathroom with his clothes.

Face palm. Why? Why would I go and mention a wedding? I was the worst at this.

Reid came out four minutes later wearing his slacks and dress shirt. His hair was mussed from my fingers yanking on it earlier, making me wish he was climbing back in bed with me instead of leaving.

"I won't be long." He dropped a kiss on my lips before walking out the door.

After two minutes of mentally beating myself up for the inept way I'd handled his offer to come with me to LA, I went and took a quick shower. Afterward, I put on my favorite T-shirt, captioned, "I licked it first. It's mine."

Deciding not to waste the time, I started packing my suitcase since we were leaving early the next morning. My task was interrupted, however, by a knock on the door. When I looked through the peephole, I was shocked to see Chance on the other side. Opening the door a crack, I told him, "Reid isn't here. He's with your mom."

"I know. I saw him in the lobby. I came to talk to you."

"If you think I'm inviting you into our room, you are sadly mistaken."

"Would you rather talk about your job at the Scarlett Letter in the hallway?"

My stomach dropped. How the hell had he discovered my secret from thousands of miles away? I opened the door to let him in and turned around so he wouldn't be able to see my reaction.

"It was the connection to Chloe that clued me in. I knew what kind of lengths Aiden went to in order to get her out of a certain auction."

Fuck, fuck, fuck.

Chloe had entered an auction for her virginity in order to pay off a dangerous loan shark. Aiden had found out about it by reading messages she'd mistakenly thought were private, and the rest was wrapped up in a happy ending for the two of them. Evidently, the same wasn't going to be said about me.

"What do you want?" I turned to face him, crossing my arms over my chest and refusing to be bullied. "Because from where I stand, it looks like it's for your brother to be miserable."

Irritation showed in his eyes. "Of course I don't want to see him miserable. But are you going to stand there and tell me you've been honest with him?"

"That's rich coming from you. You want to talk about honesty when you would go behind his back and cheat—"

"I didn't cheat. Jesus, that wasn't the point. The point was to show him the truth about Vanessa. She'd drop to her knees for me or for any other man she thought might elevate her position. And since he didn't believe me when I told him she'd hit on me, I proved it. I'm here to protect him, even from himself."

"Must be a thankless job. But you can rest easy. I'll tell Reid about the Scarlett Letter tonight." I had no choice.

"And what? Let's play this scenario out, shall we? My brother is a good guy, and I'm sure you'll tell him you work there because you need the money. Might even be a good sob story."

In other words, Chance didn't give a shit about my reasons.

"So he says he understands. And maybe you go so far as to quit your job there."

I hated him for being a step ahead of me.

"But you've met this crowd. You think he'll be able to bring you home for the holidays? Would he be able to hold his head up, aware everyone could find out like I did that you stripped illegally? He'd know people would question if you'd also been involved in prostitution because if you'd do one illegal thing, why not another? Hell, they'll wonder if Reid paid you to be here. And how do you believe your illegal activity plays out in connection with his career in security? You suppose he'll keep his clearance if your vocation were to be uncovered? You imagine he'll get that promotion in Australia he put in for?"

I bit the inside of my cheek in order to keep from showing any outward emotion and tasted blood.

"So maybe you two talk it out, but what type of future are you saddling him with?"

"I repeat, what do you want?" A man like Chance always had an agenda.

"I'll make it worth your while."

Rage threatened to make me dizzy. "You'd pay me to break up with your brother?"

"Twenty-five thousand, and you walk away with your head high and your secret intact."

"Go fuck yourself." No amount of money was worth losing Reid. Yet the voice in my head was already warning I might lose him anyhow. That was, if he'd ever been mine to lose.

His lips twitched while he handed over his card. "Very well. In case you change your mind, the offer expires at midnight, Cinderella."

I couldn't shut the door on his retreat fast enough. But once I was alone, anxiety crawled up my throat and threatened to consume me. I needed to talk to Reid. But what could I say?

Simple. I'd tell him the truth. I stripped to fund my niece's cancer treatment, but now that she was cancer-free, I intended to quit. And I wanted—what? That he shouldn't be ashamed of me? Reid might not have the best relationship with his family, but he clearly wanted them to remain in his life. Look at the way he'd left to allow his mother to apologize. Did I want Vanessa and her catty bitch posse to have the satisfaction of knowing he'd traded down?

Perhaps that was the crux of the matter. With or without the exposure of my secret, I believed Reid could do a lot better than Cheez Whiz.

Chapter Thirty-One
REID

I left the hotel room in a hurry, hoping I could quickly listen to my mother's half-ass apology, something no doubt designed to make her feel better rather than to mend fences with me. As soon as that was done, I could get back up to the room with Teagan. She'd seemed caught off guard by my offer to go to LA with her, but I hoped we could talk more about it once I returned, so I could explain how much I wanted to meet her sister and niece.

However, what I wanted above all else was a chance to see how good we could be together. And if I had to spend months convincing her that I was over my ex and safely out of rebound territory, I was up for the task.

With any luck, she would still be naked in bed upon my return to the room. I didn't think I'd ever get enough of her incredible body. But there was much more than our physical connection. She made me feel good about myself, and could make even the most mundane activities fun.

In my mind, I was already running through what I needed to do. Book a flight to LA, text Aiden and let him know I was coming, reserve a hotel room, call work and tell them I was taking a couple more days off, and romance the hell out of Teagan. But first, a few minutes of family business.

I found my mother waiting for me in the lobby. She was alone. For some reason, I'd feared this might be another attempt to get me and my ex back together, but I was relieved to see that didn't appear to be the case.

"Hello, my dear," she greeted.

"Hi."

"Thank you for meeting me."

"You're welcome."

Silence. Then I saw Vanessa approaching. Dammit. I should've listened to my instincts when they'd warned me this was a setup. "You said this was about an apology."

My mother expelled a long breath. "It is. I'm sorry about earlier. And your fiancée has an apology too."

Ex-Fiancée. I didn't want to hear any more apologies. That's what happened when you no longer cared for someone. You were no longer interested if they were sorry or not.

Vanessa came up, glancing from my mother to me. "The thought of never talking to you again, Reid—it breaks my heart."

That made one of us. I might have invested years in this woman, but I could definitely say I no longer loved her. And I had no intention of wasting another minute with her. "I need to go."

"Wait. I have the ring."

"What?"

"The engagement ring. It's supposed to get returned to you."

I'd written it off as a loss. "You want to give it back?"

"Yes. It's the right thing to do, and maybe it'll provide the closure I need."

"Okay." Such conscientiousness was unexpected from her direction.

"You'll come up to my room with me?" Sensing my hesitation, she added, "You know, your mom can accompany us if you're worried about how it'll look."

Great, two people I didn't want to spend time with. But returning the ring was a type of closure, I had to admit. Although I'd never propose to another woman with it, perhaps I could sell it and donate the money.

My mom easily complied. "Of course, I'd be happy to come up with you."

We walked toward the elevators together in an awkward silence until my mother asked, "You off to Dubai in the morning?"

"Actually, we're heading to LA. Aiden is there now, so it'll be good to see him."

"Do tell him hello. I haven't seen his mother lately. I need to call her. When is he coming home? He didn't visit this last Christmas."

No, he hadn't, the lucky bastard. Among our families, the holiday circuit was brutal, including all manner of high-society parties and other various family obligations. I was already thinking I'd like to spend the next holiday season with Teagan, taking her wherever she wanted to go. "I have no idea, but I'll be sure to ask him."

Once we were in the elevator, my mom pulled out her phone and soon started huffing as she typed.

"What's wrong?" I asked.

"My phone has been having issues. Be a dear and let me use yours to confirm my car for tonight."

I unlocked it and handed it over without a thought. Once the elevator door opened, I stepped off to follow Vanessa to her room. When she opened the door, I was surprised to see her mother. "Oh, hello, Mrs. Lane."

"Hello, dear." She cut a look to her daughter and then to my mother. Perhaps they were under the misapprehension there was a chance for reconciliation, but I'd come for the ring and nothing else.

"It's in here," Vanessa said, walking toward a bedroom.

I wasn't going to follow her until, to my relief, I spotted a ring box sitting on the desk. As I came into the room, I braced myself for one last emotional scene. I had to physically keep myself from bolding once I heard the French doors start to close behind us.

Mrs. Lane gave me a smile as I turned. "Just to give you two some privacy."

I'd never wanted to escape as badly as I did right now. I didn't owe Vanessa a thing. However, I wasn't a complete dick. If returning my ring in private provided her with closure and the ability to move on, then I could deal with a few more painful minutes. In return, I'd know I'd never have to do it again.

Chapter Thirty-Two
TEAGAN

I was about to go nuts. Where was Reid? He'd been gone almost twenty minutes. In retrospect, I supposed that, in addition to meeting his mother, he was probably saying goodbye to his friends. Damn. I should've gotten dressed again myself and gone with him.

My phone buzzed on the nightstand, and I breathed a sigh of relief at seeing Reid's name on the screen. He was probably telling me he was smoking a cigar with Phil or something. But the words I read took me off guard.

"I'm up in Vanessa's room talking. I may be a while."

My stomach had been in knots ever since Chance's visit. Now it threatened a full-on mutiny. I typed my reply quickly.

"Okay. I should've said this earlier, but I'm looking forward to going to LA together."

Given my less-than-enthusiastic response to his suggestion, I needed to ensure he understood my true wishes.

But no response. Fifteen minutes. Then twenty. Finally, unable to stand it any longer, I texted him again.

"Need a rescue?"

The dots appeared immediately, indicating he was typing.

At least you couldn't text while having sex with the ex. Unless he was getting a blowjob. Jesus. I was being paranoid, but vulnerability was tough to overcome. I couldn't help feeling uneasy. Hell, for all I knew Chance had left me to go talk to his brother. Right now, Reid could be finding out my secret from someone who couldn't explain the why.

"No rescue needed, but I'll be a while longer. I'm sorry, but I have feelings to resolve."

A gut punch would've felt better. A little voice in my mind gloated that I told you so. He hadn't promised anything, and we hadn't discussed our future.

Another text came in. **"It may be best if you go to LA alone. I should return home with Vanessa and figure things out."**

Translation. He was taking a step toward getting back together with his ex. God, how could I have been stupid enough to think he was ready to start a new relationship? To believe he'd choose me, of all people, with which to do so.

I didn't bother to respond. What could I say?

But I did have a decision to make. Stay here, pathetically hoping he'd return to the room if only to collect his things before I left for my flight tomorrow morning, or avoid any kind of awkward farewell altogether.

Avoidance reigned supreme. I had my pride. I wasn't about to let him see me cry. So I called down to the concierge and found out there was a red-eye flight to Chicago leaving at midnight. From there, I could connect to LA. It was a brutal way to get home, but at this point, I'd take it.

THE LOBBY WAS MOSTLY empty when I walked off the elevator trailing my suitcase behind me. I had my head down and intended to ask the doorman for a taxi to the airport when a now-familiar voice stopped me.

"Teagan?"

"Of course you're here, because my night just can't get worse."

Chance looked down at my suitcase. "Where are you going?"

"None of your business." The last person I wanted to spend another minute talking to was Reid's brother.

"You're leaving?"

"Nothing gets by you."

The judgy motherfucker had the audacity to look disappointed. "I'll wire your money. Just give me the account number."

My chuckle was hollow. "I don't want your fucking money. I'm leaving because Reid is evidently going home with Vanessa to resolve his feelings."

Chance's eyes went wide. "You're joking."

"Do I look like I'm in a joking mood?"

"But he's crazy about you."

"Yet you were willing to ruin that too." All my adrenaline was busy draining my body and leaving a heavy sadness in its place. "Anyhow, I'd give you a big fuck-you speech, but I'm fresh out of fucks to give."

I turned to go but felt his gentle tug on my elbow.

"Wait. Where is Reid now?"

I shrugged one shoulder. "Don't know, don't care."

Maybe if I repeated the words, I'd start to believe them. The moisture gathering in my eyes told me differently.

He muttered a curse. "Where are you heading?"

"LA."

"My private plane can take you."

"I'd rather walk barefoot across glass and fire to get to LA than share a plane with you."

His brow rose at my absurd comeback. What could I say? It wasn't my best work.

"You and your feet can rest assured; I wouldn't be with you. I'll call the pilot now and tell him to expect you."

It was tempting to tell him hell no, but that meant a middle seat on the flight to Chicago, a layover, and then another middle seat, no doubt, on the way to LA. By using Chance's plane, I could at least get there quicker. He might be doing it in order to guarantee my departure, but at this point I didn't care.

"Fine."

Chapter Thirty-Three

REID

I needed to leave. Desperately.

"And remember when we went on vacation to the Caymans together? How much fun we had?"

I ran a hand through my hair, exasperated with Vanessa's attempt to go down memory lane. She'd kept me captive for what seemed an eternity. I reached for the phone in my pocket in order to check the time, only to remember I'd given it to my mom. Shit. I couldn't even text Teagan to let her know I was held up.

"Vanessa, I can appreciate our history, but it's in the past. It's time to move forward. I need to go."

She hadn't given me the ring yet, instead cradling it in her hands as though she couldn't bear to part with it.

"Keep the ring."

"But I want to give it back."

"Then do, but either way, I'm leaving." I was already at the double doors and soon found something had been propped on the other side to block my way out. "What the hell is this?"

"Your mom and my parents—they really wish we could work things out."

"So they decided to block the doors?"

This was insane. But I suddenly recollected Imelda the psychic's words: "Don't let the past trap you." I'd thought she meant figuratively, not literally.

I surveyed the room for a hotel phone, but evidently, they'd thought to remove it. After banging on the doors, I put my weight against them. "Let me out."

"We're doing this for your own good, darling," came my mom's voice.

I turned toward Vanessa. "Tell them to let us out. Now."

"Only if you promise to fly to New Hampshire with me for a few days. We could go to couples therapy."

"I don't know how else to say this. I don't love you any longer. We are not a couple, and we will never be again. It's over."

Her face morphed into ugly-cry mode, but I was too busy trying to find an escape route to care. I walked out to the balcony and judged the distance between it and the one belonging to the room next door. An athlete I was not, but desperate times and all that.

Man dies from balcony fall while trying to get away from cheating ex-fiancée.

I could see the headline now. But as I was about to climb up and take my chances, the sound of loud voices came from the other room, and the French doors opened. Chance absorbed the situation, glancing from me to Vanessa and back again.

"I totally understand your desire to jump, but we both know athleticism was never really your forte. I think the door makes a better option."

Without a backward glance at Vanessa, I strode out. In the

living area, I glared at my mother who didn't have the good sense to look contrite over her actions. "Give me my phone."

She handed it over without a fuss, and I was out the front door with Chance on my heels. I didn't stop until I hit the elevator.

"Jesus, I knew our mother was crazy, but this is another level."

"I have a feeling it gets worse. You may want to look at your phone. Specifically, at the messages you've supposedly sent to Teagan."

Dread pooled in my belly, and I looked down. "There's nothing. Shit. Mom must've deleted the text message string. Christ, I can't find Teagan's contact info either." My phone was the only place I had Teagan's number, and I only had her work email address. I'd have to call the office to retrieve it. "I need to get to her."

"You may already be too late."

My head snapped toward Chance as the elevator doors opened onto my floor.

He had to be wrong. A series of text messages couldn't have caused Teagan to flee, no matter what they'd said. Yet my hand shook when I put my key card in our hotel room door. I walked in to find the only signs of her to be the designer clothing and shoes purposefully left behind.

Suddenly a thought slammed through my mind, and I turned to my brother. "How did you know where to find me? How did you know Teagan would be gone and that Mom had tampered with my phone? Were you in on this?"

Chance shook his head. "Of course not. You think I want to see you with Vanessa? No way. But what I'm about to tell you won't make you happy either."

Chapter Thirty-Four
TEAGAN

The beauty I found in taking a private jet was bypassing the entire airport and instead taking a car straight to the waiting plane.

Part of me wondered if there'd be a catch. With Chance, I was sure there always would be, but when I boarded, the pilots and single flight attendant were ready for me. I didn't bother to appreciate the opulent leather seats, the state-of-the-art entertainment system, or the full bar at my disposal.

Before long, we took off. After accepting a bottle of water from the flight attendant, I effectively dismissed her for the rest of the flight. I was probably the lowest-maintenance passenger she'd ever had on this plane.

I'd been tempted to call Chloe or my sister, but what would I say? I was heartbroken because I'd agreed to become a fake date for a guy I knew wasn't over his ex-fiancée, and now I was shocked to learn he wasn't over her? Or better yet, how about his older brother finding out I was a stripper in a country where it was illegal—then offering to pay me to leave Reid alone. Good times.

At least I was over my crush. Of course, it had cost me my heart to get here.

As the plane flew toward LA, I did what I'd done my entire life. I internalized it all. Beat myself up about letting my guard down, and for believing for one minute my infatuation could become a real-life relationship. My eyes burned with hot tears.

Stupid girl.

Served me right for getting my hopes up and starting to believe there could be such a thing as a happy ending. And hell, maybe there was, but not for a girl like me. I'd made my choices. I owned them. And if people wanted to judge me for them, then they could fuck right off.

IT WAS early morning when the Uber dropped me off in front of my sister's apartment complex. I'd sent her a text just saying, "here early, will be there soon." But weirdly I'd had no reply. Perhaps she was on another job interview or with Penelope at a doctor's appointment. They'd had one on Friday, and I wondered how it had gone.

I had a key but chose to knock since she hadn't answered my text. I was unprepared for the devastated look on my sister's face when she opened the door.

She immediately went in for a hug and burst into tears. My sister didn't hug or cry. Ever. Except once. When Penelope had first been diagnosed with leukemia. Oh, no.

"What happened at the appointment?"

She pulled away, wiping her eyes as if she was angry with the tears for falling. "It's back. The cancer. Or it never left. I don't know. They're scheduling another round of chemo beginning later this week."

My heavy sigh fell between us. I couldn't think of worse news.

"Sorry. Come in. You must be tired. Why are you here early? I wasn't expecting you until later tonight."

I followed her inside with my suitcase. "There was an earlier flight available." I wouldn't tell her what had happened with Reid. My problems paled in comparison to what she was going through. What my niece was going through. "You found out on Friday?"

"I did. And don't be mad I didn't tell you right away. You were at the wedding, and I figured it would be a better conversation to have in person."

I wouldn't debate her. "Where is Penelope?"

"Napping."

I took a seat on the secondhand couch and tried not to let the shittiness of the world overwhelm me. It would do no good to wallow. "How did she take the news?"

Tory took a seat next to me, heaving out a sigh. "She took the news like a champ. Said she was sad her hair wouldn't get a chance to grow back yet, but she'd stay strong and fight it again."

The last word came on a broken whisper, causing a tear to slip down my face. Four fucking years old and trying to be strong and fight cancer.

"God, I have to get myself together. I've had no luck in getting a new job. Not sure how I'll get one now with all of the appointments I'll have to take Penny to."

Tory stripped at a local club a few nights a week, earning enough money to pay rent and cover food costs, but not leaving much left over for medical care or anything extra. She'd tried to get a day job, but it was impossible to balance a nine-to-five with a sick child who needed daily medical care. Sure, if she'd already been in a job for a year, she could have qualified for FMLA, Family Medical Leave Act, but that wasn't the case.

As much as I'd have loved to quit my job at the Scarlett Letter—and had planned to do so—this took priority. "I'll take more shifts at the club." Myra, the woman in charge, was always flexible with girls who requested more hours. I'd even endure more back-room dances if I had to.

"I can't ask you to do that. How are things with your boss going? How was the wedding? You can't jeopardize anything with him by continuing to work there."

"I wouldn't be jeopardizing anything with Reid. It's over. Or it didn't really begin. He's still hung up on his ex."

Her eyes didn't leave mine. "Men suck."

"Yes, they do, but maybe going with him for the weekend had been necessary, so I could get over my crush once and for all." Getting over heartbreak would be tougher, but I'd throw myself into the club and numb myself to the rest.

"Will working for him be awkward?"

I hadn't gotten that far in my plans for the future, but I'd deal with it the way I dealt with any emotionally distressing situation. By pretending it didn't affect me. I was well-versed in the art. "Probably, but I can transfer to another department. Also, he's most likely moving to the Sydney office in the next couple of months anyhow. I suppose it's all worked out the way it should."

Her scrutiny was unnerving. "But you got hurt in the process?"

"Yep. But I'm fine." I would be. Eventually.

She took my hand in hers. "I'm sorry."

"Me too. Anyway, I'll return to Dubai tomorrow. Take some extra shifts if I have to, but we'll get through it." I had a measure of regret over leaving most of my expensive clothes behind in the hotel room. I could've sold them if I'd been thinking clearly.

Her eyes teared up again. "I don't want you to have to take extra shifts."

"Tough shit. I'm not doing it for you. I'm doing it for the bravest little four-year-old on the planet."

"You were supposed to see Chloe and have some days off."

"She will understand." If anyone would, it would be Chloe. "All you need to focus on is getting the best care you can for Penny. Have you thought about getting a second opinion?"

"I think about it, but the options are limited once they hear you don't have insurance. I wish I could get her into Children's Hospital."

"We'll get through this. She'll beat it."

She would. There was no other option my brain could fathom.

My sister, my niece, and I spent the evening watching both *Frozen* and *Frozen II*, eating pizza and popcorn, and drinking lemonade. I was out the front door at four o'clock the next morning.

With excellent timing, Chloe pulled up at the curb.

I met her with a hug when she got out to pop the back hatch of her SUV. "I don't know what I did to deserve such an amazing friend."

She shook her head. "Please, if taking you to the airport is the only time I get to spend with you, then I don't care how early I have to come to pick you up."

"Thank you."

We got into the car, and she put it into gear before the questions started. "What's going on with Reid? He's been blowing up Aiden's phone since last night. He says he's on his way here. Something about his mom using his phone to send you messages about getting back together with his ex."

"What?" Reid hadn't sent the messages? He wasn't reconciling with his ex?

"Yeah, crazy. But I did what you asked. I told him I hadn't heard from you and didn't know your plans. But, Teagan, please call him."

Hope bloomed in my chest followed by a piercing shot of regret. "I can't."

"What happened between you two?"

There was a lot to catch her up on. But by the time we pulled up to the international terminal at LAX, I'd given my best shot at relaying most of it.

"So you saw the text messages and left, but now you know it wasn't him who sent them."

"Yes, but I'm sure by now Chance has told him about the club."

"So what? Aiden knew about me stripping, and it pissed him off to discover I was putting myself at risk, but it didn't change how he viewed me. And as much as I'd hate for his family to find out, it wouldn't change the way he feels about me."

"This is different. I have no intention of quitting the club. Penelope's cancer has returned."

She sucked in a breath. "I'm so sorry. Let me speak to Aiden. We could help."

I knew Aiden had money just like Reid did, but I'd never take a dime. "Even if I was tempted to accept help, my sister wouldn't touch it. She absolutely refuses to take charity."

Chloe's shoulders slumped. "There has to be a way. Talk to Reid."

"A relationship with him wouldn't work."

"Why not?"

"For one, he's told me countless times how happy he was not to be dating anyone. For another, my stripping would be a liability for him and his career. And there's the fact we're from two very different backgrounds."

"I call bullshit. Those are excuses. The type you tell yourself because you don't believe you deserve something good in your life."

"It's reality, Chloe Bear. Like I told you before, I'm Cheez Whiz, and he's spent his entire life surrounded by brie." And I'd been stupid to forget it. "Anyhow, I'll text you once I get back and let you know I arrived safely. Okay?"

She sighed but let the subject drop. "Okay."

Nineteen hours later, I walked into my apartment in Dubai, leery of what I might find. I was immediately grateful to discover I was still without a new roommate. Thank God for small favors. After a shower, I sent quick texts to my sister and Chloe to let them know I'd arrived and that I'd call them both tomorrow.

I cursed at the low-battery sign. Just my luck. I'd forgotten my charger in the resort hotel room. To conserve what power I had left until I could buy a new charger, I turned the device off. As much as I needed a nap, I had no time. I had to get to the club.

Myra didn't bat a fake eyelash when I came in that same night and asked to work during the week. The additional hours increased my risk of discovery, but what choice did I have? Dubai might be progressive, as far as Middle Eastern cities went, but there was no way it would ever be legal here for a woman to take off her clothes in a public place.

I knew exactly why I had the risks on my mind tonight. Because of Reid's brother. The fact he knew my secret unnerved me. Now I was wondering how many other people knew. And how the hell had he found out? I wished I'd thought to ask.

After changing over into my G-string and pasties, I shoved my regular clothes into my locker along with my purse. Then I turned around and took a deep breath. Another night, another dollar.

A typical evening consisted of performing a stage show, after which we'd work the crowd. It was a good thing it was a slower Wednesday night, since I wasn't on my A game. When the floor manager came up to me, I tensed, worried he'd noticed my lack of enthusiasm. Men didn't drop thousands of dollars here in order to have a lame lap dance.

"Ruby, you have a back-room request."

I wasn't over my last back-room request which had ended with me taking a backhand across the face. I was about to pass when he made my decision for me. "Myra says it's nonnegotiable."

Crap. "Which room?"

"Room six."

I didn't like the idea of meeting a mystery man in room six, but it wasn't unusual for a customer to see you on the floor and request your presence in a private room. Hopefully, he wouldn't be creepy or horrible like the Russian man from two weeks ago.

But when I walked into room six, I faced my worst nightmare.

Chapter Thirty-Five

REID

"What the hell did you do? What won't I like?" My brother was a lot of things, but a liar wasn't one of them. If he said he didn't have a hand in locking me in with Vanessa, I believed him. But there was something else he was hesitating about telling me.

"You may want to sit down for this."

I crossed over to my suitcase and began to toss clothes in. "I'm not sitting down for anything. I need to find out where Teagan is heading."

"You may not want to follow her, once I tell you what I discovered."

I moved to the closet, ripping my clothes down from the hangers. While I was at it, I grabbed the expensive dresses Teagan had left behind. "Spit it out, Chance. I have no patience for the cryptic bullshit."

"Fine. I found out Teagan is stripping at a club in Dubai."

I paused, swallowing hard at the unexpected news. "And you know this how?"

"Because I've invested money in the place."

Of course he had. Chance owned or was invested in

dozens of ventures all over the world. "What did you do with that information?"

"I confronted her with it. Told her I wouldn't disclose her moonlighting job to you or anyone else if she took twenty-five grand and left."

My heart sank while my brain fought against the idea Teagan would take a payout. "What did she do?"

"Told me to fuck off. I later noticed her in the lobby with her suitcase and asked where she was going. She told me you were heading back to New Hampshire to work things out with Vanessa. I knew that couldn't be true, so I found out where Vanessa's room was, and you know what happened after that."

"Shit. I don't know if Teagan would have gone to LA or Dubai."

"She went to LA. I gave her the use of my plane. Unfortunately, it took me longer than I expected to find out Vanessa's room number, so it's already taken off."

I turned to face him. "Why would you offer her use of your plane?"

He suddenly looked uncomfortable. "Because she seemed upset, and I'm not a complete asshole all the time."

That was the thing it was sometimes hard to remember about Chance. Despite his best attempts to act the contrary, I'd seen slivers of his decency our entire lives. "Did offering her the plane ease your guilty conscience about making her feel like shit?"

"I'm not the only one with that honor. You not only allowed Mom free run of your phone, but you also decided—what? You needed another dramatic scene with Vanessa up in her room?"

I hated that he had a point. Pinching the bridge of my nose, I wished I could go back in time and change that decision. "Vanessa wanted to return the ring. In hindsight, I should've told her to keep it. But I was trying to—I don't know—give her some closure."

"No, you were once again putting other people's feelings above your own. See where it gets you?"

Chance had always been critical of what he called my bleeding heart. In this case, it turned out he wasn't wrong.

"You're truly over her, though, aren't you?"

I closed the drawers and threw more clothes into my suitcase. "One hundred percent."

"I can have another plane here in a few hours to fly us to LA."

"I'm not going anywhere with you. Teagan had the right idea by telling you to fuck off."

His jaw clenched. "She passed the test by not taking the money."

My seldom-seen temper snapped. "There was no test she needed to pass, you prick. Not with me, and especially not with you."

"So you're okay with her stripping? In a country where it's illegal, by the way. She may need the money, but will you be cool about bringing her to family functions if anyone finds out where she moonlights?"

"God, you're such a judgmental prick. You can own and operate strip clubs, but the girls who work there aren't worthy, is that it?"

Her stripping didn't affect the way I felt about her, especially since I had a good idea of why she was doing it. But I did care about the jeopardy she put herself in each night she did so. Suddenly, I remembered the bruise she'd been trying to hide. Jesus. The thought of how she might actually have gotten it made my stomach sick.

"I never said she isn't worthy. But she didn't tell you

about the stripping. And if she's involved in one illegal activity, she may be involved in more."

I ignored Chance's ridiculous assertion. "This must have to do with her four-year-old niece's cancer treatment and sending money home to her sister."

"I'm sure that's what she told you, but do you believe—?"

"You're a cynical son of a bitch. Yes, I believe her. Now go away. I have things to do, and I don't need you questioning my every move and trying to tear apart a person who has done nothing to deserve it."

He heaved a heavy sigh. "I can help you."

My eyes met his. "No. You can't. You've done nothing but try to undermine and destroy my relationships. And you can tell yourself all day long you are trying to protect me, but you know what? I think you enjoy being a bully."

His brow furrowed. "Did it ever occur to you if I hadn't pushed the issue with your ex-fiancée, you never would've had a relationship with Teagan?"

Of course it had, and it was a bitter pill to swallow. "You want me to—what? Thank you?"

"I saved you from a future with a woman who would've made your life miserable."

"You're right, she would have. But you could've come talk to me instead of doing what you did. Instead, you destroyed my relationship with you as well." And for the first time I realized the damage to our bond had been what hurt the most.

His eyes went wide. "I tried to tell you she'd hit on me. You wouldn't listen."

He was right. He had come to me a year ago. And I'd made excuses. She'd flirted because she'd been drunk, she hadn't meant the words, and he must've been mistaken. I'd foolishly given her the benefit of the doubt.

He sighed heavily. "I had a window to finally prove how unworthy she was, and I took it. I'm sorry it hurt you in the process as I only ever wanted what was best for you."

"Teagan is what's best for me. She's everything I didn't realize I was missing in my life."

Neither of us spoke for the longest minute. Finally, he said, "Then let me help you fix it. Please."

I considered his request as I finished packing up my things, along with the items Teagan left behind, and zipped up my suitcase. As much as I'd love to tell him to go to hell, there was a desperation and sincerity in his tone which had me pausing. In addition, his private plane would expedite things, being much faster than flying commercial.

"Fine."

Unfortunately, Chance wasn't able to get another pilot until the next morning, putting me hours behind Teagan when we landed in Los Angeles that afternoon. Although I'd obtained Teagan's cell phone number again via the office, my calls and text messages went unanswered. Either she had my number blocked, or her phone was turned off.

Unfortunately, I'd hit a dead end. Teagan was undoubtedly staying with her sister, but I didn't have the address. We put Chance's private investigator on the problem, but he didn't come through until ten minutes before I got a text from Aiden. Chloe had just dropped Teagan off at the airport.

"Shit. Teagan is on her way back to Dubai," I said to my brother. Why the quick turnaround? Was this all to avoid me?

Chance was already dialing his phone. "That long of a trip will take two pilots and a few hours to arrange, but we can drive to the airport now."

Part of me was tempted to book a commercial flight and leave my brother here in LA, but if he was committed to helping me, then I wouldn't turn it down. I had to get to Teagan.

We took off within four hours and arrived in Dubai sixteen hours later.

"I take it you'll try Teagan's apartment first?" Chance asked as we deplaned.

"Yes. It's a weeknight, so she ought to be there. And you're coming with me."

I'd never seen him rendered speechless, but he was now. I answered his unasked question. "You owe her a spectacular apology. One that includes assurance you won't ever mention the club to her or anyone else ever again. And if we have any hope of salvaging a brotherly relationship in the future, you'd better do anything it takes to ensure she accepts your apology. Because if I have to choose between my family and her, it's an easy choice."

I wouldn't allow her to feel bullied or threatened ever again.

His expression was solemn. "I'll do anything it takes. You have my word."

Thirty minutes later, we arrived at Teagan's door. Shit. She either wasn't answering her doorbell, or she wasn't home. Given there was no light showing under the door and that I didn't see her red Jeep in the parking lot, I was going with the latter of the two.

Chance hung up his phone, looking grim. "Come on. I know where she is."

Chapter Thirty-Six
TEAGAN

I stepped through to room number six and stopped in my tracks. "No fucking way. I will quit on the spot before my ass gets anywhere near your lap."

Chance rolled his eyes and threw a blob of material at me. "Put this on."

It was a silk robe, black in color. "I don't know what kind of kink you're into, but—"

"Jesus, and here I was the one accused of being cynical. The robe is to cover yourself before Reid walks through the door."

"He's here now?" Instant panic propelled me to throw the robe on quickly.

"Yes, and since I figured you'd rather be covered when you see him, I bought us a couple minutes."

I lifted my chin. So the jig was up, and Reid knew I was here. "I don't care how he sees me."

"Bullshit."

Maybe, but hell if I'd ever show it. "How did you know I was here?"

"I'm one of the club's investors."

Of course. Now it made sense how he'd found out about me.

Two knocks sounded on the door before it opened. Once I laid eyes on Reid, all of my false bravado evaporated.

My arms crossed over my chest as I fought both tears and an overwhelming urge to flee. It wasn't merely uncomfortable to have my two worlds collide; it was cruel.

"Hi." Reid looked tired and unbelievably handsome in a rumpled button-down and slacks.

"Hi."

He glanced at his brother. "Can you give us some privacy?"

"Certainly. I'll be outside the door."

"I can't stay back here long. They'll be expecting me on the floor soon." It was a flimsy excuse, but I had to try something to shorten the impending conversation.

Chance paused on his way out. "It's been cleared. Take your time."

So much for my escape plan. As soon as the door closed, I went on the offensive. "What the hell are you doing here?"

"I needed to talk to you. I know you received some text messages, but they weren't actually from me. My mother asked to use my phone to call for a car, but evidently used it to text you some fake messages. Before that happened, Vanessa claimed she wanted to return the engagement ring. I didn't put two and two together until after it was too late. By then, my mother and Vanessa's had barricaded me into a hotel room with her. I was ready to leap from the balcony to the one next door when Chance stormed in. Otherwise, I'd probably have broken my neck."

"Trapped by your past," I whispered. The fact the psychic's words had come true sent a shiver down my spine.

"Who would've thought it was a direct warning against kidnapping?"

Although Chloe had already said the whole string of text messages had been a misunderstanding, I'd needed to hear it from him. "So you weren't ever working it out with Vanessa? Or returning to New Hampshire with her?"

"No way. Not remotely close. I took her up on her offer to return the engagement ring because my mother came up to her room with me. Foolishly, I couldn't imagine what could go wrong. The entire time I was stuck there, I was anxious to return to you. And I can't tell you how many times I've kicked myself for giving in to Vanessa and letting her talk me into giving her 'closure.'"

"I appreciate the explanation, but it doesn't matter." My voice was full of misery. Having given up on anger, I went straight for resigned. He wasn't with his ex, but here I was in a strip club. The end result was the same.

"Because of Chance? You don't need to worry about him. He won't ever tell anyone else or threaten you again."

"Good. Um, I should get back to work. But I appreciate you coming by and clearing things up."

His eyes went wide. "Maybe I'm doing this all wrong. I chased you to LA and then here because I want to be with you."

Whoosh went my emotions. God, I wanted to be with him too. "You can't be in a relationship with a stripper—especially not in a country where taking your clothes off in public is illegal. Think about it, Reid. I could jeopardize your clearance, your promotions, your career. Hell, you being here right now has already put it all in jeopardy."

He ran a hand through his hair. "I don't understand. I assumed you took this job, with its associated risk, in order to help pay for your niece's cancer treatment."

"Yes."

"But she's now in remission."

"Was in remission." My voice cracked on the last word.

"Jesus. It's back?"

I didn't trust my voice, so I nodded instead.

"I'll pay for whatever treatment she needs. Then she can get the necessary care, and you can quit this job."

Of course he would offer to do so. It was the type of man he was. It broke my heart to turn him down. "Even if I wanted to take you up on your offer, my sister never would. She has a hard enough time taking money from me."

"She'd rather you continue taking this risk? Maybe get some more bruises on your face for your trouble?"

Thankfully, the lights were dim enough to hide the tears springing to my eyes. Of course he'd figured out the lie I'd told him. "I'm sure she wouldn't ask me to. But her daughter is battling cancer. And she's trying to juggle numerous doctor and chemo appoints with a job to keep food on the table and a roof over their heads—a job that doesn't give medical benefits. We're already in a good deal of debt from the first round."

My heart sank when Reid walked over to the door and opened it. He was leaving, and I couldn't blame him. It was too much for him.

Chance stood at the open door. "We ready to go?" he asked, looking between us.

Reid shook his head and spoke in low tones until Chance focused his gaze on me.

"This problem is easily remedied," Chance said. "I'll simply give your sister a job with health benefits. Now, are we ready to go?"

"You can just give her a job?"

"Of course. I'll fly out tomorrow and talk to her myself."

A kernel of hope took hold. Tory was stubborn, but she was also practical and would do anything for her daughter. If she had a job with medical benefits, there'd be a lot less to pay out of pocket. I might still have to work a second job to help out, but I wouldn't have to do it here at the club. "The job would need to be flexible about hours since she has to go to so many appointments for her daughter."

"I'll make sure it's flexible."

"She'll be prideful, so you'll have to make it a real job offer."

Chance scoffed. "You sorely underestimate my ability to get what I want."

Reid stared down his brother. "You owe Teagan something."

Chance took a deep breath, looking deeply uneasy. "I owe you an apology. I was trying to protect Reid, and I went way too far. I'm sorry I questioned your intentions and judged you before knowing anything about you."

His words rang sincere. "If you promise to never mention this place again and you're serious about the job you'll offer for my sister, then I accept your apology."

He gave a curt nod. "Consider it done. Now, are we ready to go?"

Chapter Thirty-Seven
REID

My relief was palpable once we were in Teagan's Jeep, and the club was in our rearview mirror. She was safe. She was with me. Not in the way I wanted, but hopefully we could remedy that soon.

We didn't talk until we started walking up to her apartment. "No roommate yet, I take it?"

"Yeah, lucky for me."

Once we were inside, the awkwardness between us felt disheartening. I wished I knew what she was thinking. Only one way to find out.

"What's running through your beautiful head?"

She turned toward me as we both stood in her kitchen. A touch of vulnerability showed on her face. "I never wanted you to see me the way you did tonight. In the club."

Her jeans and T-shirt made it hard to remember she'd been in the dark, back room of an illegal strip club a half hour ago.

I stepped closer to her, tucking her hair behind her ear. It was curly again, making me smile. "I get why you didn't want me to see you there, but I'm glad I did. That place showed me the full picture of what you've been going through to pay for your niece's medical care. And although I absolutely don't want you returning to the club because I worry about the danger you put yourself in, I understand why you did it. But now, thankfully, you have other options."

"You're assuming your brother won't be an asshole and Tory won't tell him to fuck off before he even gets a chance to offer a job."

"He'll tone it down and figure out something. He has a lot riding on it."

Her brow tipped up. "How so?"

"I told him the only way for redemption was to make things right with you. And the way he makes it right with you is both to apologize and to get your sister to take the job. He'll either succeed, or he'll make himself completely miserable trying. It's kind of a win-win. You don't think she'll let pride rule her decision, do you?"

"No. I think ultimately she'll take the job because it's what's best for my niece."

"Will you call her and give her a heads-up?"

She contemplated. "I probably should."

"Please don't worry. Chance is the most persuasive guy I know."

She rolled her eyes. "I have my doubts, but let's hope in this case he is."

"I'm sorry I went up to Vanessa's room to get the ring. It was stupid to give her any more of my time. And I'm sorry for the text messages. I don't know what they said, but obviously they, coupled with my brother's asshole offer, made you leave. I tried to text and call you."

She reached to her purse and pulled out her phone. "I kept

it off because I'm down to five percent battery. I forgot my charger in the resort hotel room."

Now I knew why she hadn't answered any of my messages. She hadn't even received them.

She powered her phone on and handed it over.

After I scrolled upward from all of my new messages, I read the ones my mother had sent to Teagan as me, instantly feeling anger toward her interference.

"My mother deleted your phone number from my phone. I guess it was a silly delay tactic, hoping you would leave, and I wouldn't be able to reach you quickly enough to tell you what really happened." I sighed, handing her phone back to her.

"Yeah, but it worked."

"I have to ask you something. Why, after everything that had happened between us, would you believe I would get back together with Vanessa?" I guessed the answer, but I wanted to hear how she explained it.

"After the visit from your brother, I was anxious and on edge, not knowing how I was going to tell you about the strip club. By the time these text messages came in, it wasn't hard to convince me of anything. We fessed up to our attraction to each other, had sex, and it was great, but you didn't make me any promises. Hell, if anything, you were very clear that you weren't ready for another relationship and were trying to avoid a rebound."

My hand reached out to take hers. "The night of the rehearsal dinner, Vanessa came up to me, and I didn't feel anything except annoyance. Time with her meant keeping me from you. I knew then I was completely over her and ready for a fresh start."

Teagan's eyes went wide. "You never shared that."

"I know. My plan, which now sounds stupid, was to get

far away from the wedding weekend and my ex, and put some distance between us and our fake relationship. I thought when we went to LA, or maybe once we were back here in Dubai, just the two of us, I could tell you how I wanted this to be real."

Chapter Thirty-Eight
TEAGAN

My heart was racing, and hope was ready to leak out of my eyes in the form of tears if I wasn't careful. But insecurity reigned supreme and was not ready to let me accept his words.

"Reid, even if I quit the club, I'm not the type of girl you want to bring home to your family or who will make the best impression at a business dinner."

"You'd make an amazing impression by just being yourself. Do you even realize what a breath of fresh air you are? You've always been unapologetic about who you are, so don't go apologizing now."

"How can you say that to me? You spent so much time prepping, molding me into the version of a girlfriend you wanted people to see at the wedding, from the designer clothes to the fake background. I even had to have a separate pair of shoes for every outfit because, oh, the horror of wearing the same pair twice."

His mouth opened and closed. Finally, he found the words. "I bought the clothes and shoes because I didn't want you to have to deal with any judgment from the people at the wedding. We were only supposed to be faking things, so I just wanted you to feel like you could fit in with that crowd over the weekend. In hindsight—I'm sorry. I never cared what you wore. I only cared that you should feel comfortable in the face of extreme cattiness. As for the fake background about your parents and education, that was your idea. I went with it because your true history was nobody's business, and I didn't want you to be in a vulnerable position with respect to the assholes I knew would be in attendance. I moved over six thousand miles away in order to leave behind the materialistic trappings of the world I grew up in. The last thing I want in my life is another woman like Vanessa. If for a moment you thought I could ever be embarrassed by your past or what you'd wear, then fuck—I really screwed this up."

"You didn't screw it up. I guess I didn't consider your perspective."

He framed my face with his hands. "I've never in my life had a connection like I have with you, Teagan. You not only make it easy to be with you, but you also make it easy to be myself. That's something I never had until I met you."

"It's easy to be with you too. But you can't date someone who dropped out of high school, barely got her GED, and takes her clothes off for money." I hated the insecurity reflected in my words.

"The hell I can't. I don't give a rat's ass about your education or what you did in order to earn the money for your niece's treatment. If anything, I'm in awe of how incredible you are. I wouldn't wish your upbringing on anyone, but it's clear it's made you the strong woman I see before me."

"Well, most of the time that 'strong woman' is a big old act." It was the first time I'd ever admitted it out loud.

He smiled. "I'm well aware of your tough-girl act, but I'm also aware of the sweet—" Kiss. "—soft—" Kiss. "—but fierce—" Kiss. "—passionate—" Kiss. "—sexy as hell—" Kiss. "—loyal—" Kiss. "—hates shopping, expensive luggage, and mornings side of you. Sarcasm may be your armor to keep people from getting close to you, but I promise your heart is safe with me."

Butter in the hot sun stood a better chance than I did against melting with his words.

"Where do we go from here?" I had no clue how to proceed in a relationship.

"Maybe we can talk about next steps, now that we've got all of our secrets behind us—" He paused, probably noticing the guilt I could feel registering on my face. "It is the last secret, right?"

I stepped back to give him a sheepish grin. "Um, it's not a big secret per se. In the scheme of things, I consider it more of a confession."

"What confession?"

It was time to put it all out there. "I may have had a teeny, tiny crush on you over the last year."

His eyes widened. "How tiny are we talking?"

"Scale of one to ten?"

"Sure."

"Ten, with stalkerish tendencies upgrading the package to a twelve point five."

His immediate laughter was a relief, as was the way his eyes danced with amusement as he captured my lips. "I didn't have a clue. I guess I'm flattered, and a little surprised, considering you had to stage an intervention for me."

"You bounced back pretty quickly into the Reid I adored."

"You know what they say about crushes. They typically end with a letdown."

"I've yet to find one."

"Good to know. What else is on your mind?"

"I struggle to believe good things can happen to me. And as previously discussed, I don't know if I have the tools to manage a relationship."

He leaned in, his nose below my ear. "How about I give you some options," he whispered. "Would that ease your mind?"

Was it any wonder I was gone for this man? He got me. I'd never connected with anyone else on the same level. "I could go for some options."

Smiling, he leaned back again. "Okay. Option A is we continue to date. We hang out together, laugh, kiss, and enjoy time together without any talk about the future. I earn your trust, and we baby step into what I hope will become a relationship at some point."

It sounded reasonable. It sounded safe. But it didn't sound like enough. "And option B?'

"Are you sure you can handle hearing option B? Because I can't unsay it once I've put it out there."

I nodded, grinning at the fact he was giving me an option for my options. "Lay it on me."

"Option B is the one where I tell you that in a single moment of clarity, I knew everything I've ever wanted, and didn't even know I was searching for, was right there in front of me with big green eyes and fiery red hair. There's no question in my mind I'm ready for a fresh start with you. I have no more desire to dwell on the past nor to waste one more minute on anyone from it. I'm falling in love with you, Teagan. Without a doubt in my mind. And that means I'm all in to see where this goes with you."

Holy shit.

"But know that if you choose option A, and we ease into this, we're going to slow roll into B. We will definitely get there—of that I have no doubt."

"I'm falling in love with you too." I face palmed myself. "God, that is so lame after all the beautiful words you shared. But I've never said anything like that to anyone, unless you count my sister and my niece." I'd never trusted my heart would be safe with anyone besides them. I'd never believed another person wouldn't end up letting me down.

I could see him swallow. "There's nothing lame about your words. You have a hard time believing things, especially good things, can happen to you."

Yup. Just call me Miss Belief. "What happens if you get to know me better, and you no longer like me?"

He feigned a serious expression. "Ah. Are you talking about your snoring?"

"I don't snore." Shit. "Do I?"

"You do, but it's cute at this stage. And you know what? If, years from now, it becomes intolerable, I'll simply smother you in your sleep, and we'll both agree we had a good run of it."

My laughter bubbled up. "I'm being serious."

"No, you're not. You're being scared. And the Teagan I know is brave. So put on your big-girl panties, the pink ones preferably, face your fears, and believe me when I say I'm in this one hundred percent."

I swallowed the lump in my throat, suddenly overcome by emotion. He'd hit the nail on the head. I was scared. Scared to trust someone could love me for just being me. Scared I wasn't good enough, and he'd figure out I was a fake and leave. But wait. He already knew about the falsely courageous front I put on. He already knew about my background and insecurities.

The cards were on the table, and he was choosing to play instead of walking away. For the first time, I believed his words about being all in, and I was also starting to believe I deserved them.

"How's your back?"

His brow furrowed. "What?"

"Your back? Any pain or old injuries I should be aware of?"

He looked at me like I was crazy. He wasn't wrong. "My back is fine."

"Good." Carrying out an act I'd only seen in movies, I hopped up and wrapped my legs around him. His grunt of surprise made me laugh, but the way his strong arms hoisted me up further was impressive. "I have an important question."

"What's that?" he asked, carrying me into the bedroom.

"Now that we're dating, can we have sex on your desk at work?"

He groaned. "Absolutely not."

My lip stuck out in a fake pout. "What if hot desk sex is one of my fantasies?"

His hands attacked my clothing. "We can have hot desk sex after I'm no longer your boss."

"Is desk sex still as hot if you're not my boss?" I mean, it was a legitimate question.

He stopped, staring me in the eyes. "One time."

"Deal. I'll wear no panties tomorrow, and you can call me in for oral dic-tation." I waggled my brows, causing us both to erupt into laughter.

"As much as it pains me, you probably can't keep working for me now."

"It might be short term either way if you get the job and move to Sydney."

Dammit, brain. Shut up and be happy. But I couldn't. Not so long as I still feared he might not include me in his plans.

His eyes locked on mine. "I would only take the job in Sydney if you decided to come with me."

"Really?"

"Absolutely. You chose option B, which means we're in a relationship and make decisions together about things like where to move and live. Of course, it may be hard to get Cheez Whiz in Sydney, although not any harder than here in Dubai. I suppose we could always have it shipped in. Not sure if you knew, but it's my favorite."

My eyes went wide while my mouth could only manage one word. "How?"

"Aiden slipped me a hint about what you said to Chloe. For the record, I can't stand brie. So what do you say? Can I be the nacho chip to your Cheez Whiz? The Philly cheesesteak to your—"

I held a finger to his lips. God, he really was in this a hundred percent.

"You had me at nacho chip."

He chuckled, leaning down to capture my lips.

His kiss was everything. A promise. A dream. A reality. But most of all, it was mine. All mine.

EPILOGUE

Teagan

My arms reached across the bed to find Reid's spot cool to the touch. While I was not a morning person, it turned out my boyfriend—would I ever get tired of that word?—was an early riser. It was one of many things I'd learned about him over the last eight months. And because it was a Saturday morning, I could guess where he was. Gone to pick us up fresh bagels and coffee. It had become his traditional weekend ritual since we'd moved to Sydney together.

After he returned, we'd lounge around in bed or play video games, in between having sex, of course. Finally, we'd make our way to the local market, shop for the week, and make lunch together. It turned out Reid was a great cook. Our weekend nights consisted of date nights as well as at-home movie marathons. Funny, I'd come to love some of the black-and-white classics Reid had grown up with, and he tolerated binging with me on *The Gilmore Girls* and *Supernatural*.

I missed seeing him during the day at the office, but our daily separation was for a good reason. While Reid was enjoying his new promotion as the Regional Director of Commercial Accounts for Delmont Security, I was taking classes to get my certification to work as an esthetician in Australia. In between classes, I was working some hours at a spa to pick up practical working knowledge. I'd never been happier or more in my element.

It felt strange to have my weekends off when I'd had to take on a second job for most of my life, but I no longer had to worry about paying for my niece's treatment. I couldn't wait to see her and my sister, not to mention my other LA friends when Reid and I traveled there tomorrow for the holidays.

We loved Australia and planned on exploring all the country had to offer over the next three years. After that, well, we hadn't made plans, but so long as we were together, I was game for any adventure life had to offer.

I sat up in bed when I heard the front door open and close again. When Reid walked into the bedroom of our rented apartment, I could swear my heart did a legitimate pitter-patter. What could I say? I was fucking crazy for this guy.

"Good morning, beautiful."

"Good morning to you. Bagel run?"

He walked toward the bed with a box that smelled decidedly better than bagels. "Cinnamon rolls. And here's your coffee."

"You spoil me." It wasn't an exaggeration. His thoughtfulness was only one of many reasons I loved him. I never took a single gesture of his for granted.

He sat on the bed to hand me my coffee, first giving me a kiss, morning breath be damned. "You make it easy to want to spoil you. You all packed?"

We both laughed at the absurdity of his question. Of course I wasn't packed. Reid, on the other hand, had made a list in an Excel spreadsheet and had started packing over a week ago. We might differ in so many ways, and yet our relationship worked on so many levels.

"I don't suppose you made one of those lists for me, so I'll know what to pack?"

His grin was sheepish. "If I did, am I the hero or the nerd for doing so?"

I leaned toward him, placing my hand on his handsome face. "Both. I'll have you know your dual character is one of the many reasons I love you."

"I love you too."

Gah. I'd never grow tired of those words. "I'll pack as soon as I'm done eating."

"Mm, how about after eating and after taking a shower together?"

"Deal."

The next morning we boarded the flight, this time in our own private flight cabin. It was beyond luxurious. "You know I would've been more than content with business class."

Reid grinned. "What if I said the mile-high club was one of my fantasies?"

"Oh, yeah?" Our cabin would give us plenty of privacy. "I'd say so long as they still bring me my ramekin of salted nutty perfection, I'll gladly fulfill your fantasy, Mr. Maxwell."

"I wouldn't dream of denying you your nuts."

I excused myself to the restroom, but upon returning was happy to see my nuts had arrived, along with a bottle of champagne and two flutes. Leave it to Reid to make the romantic gesture.

REID

I felt an abundance of nerves, but mostly, I was full of excitement. There were plenty of ways to propose, but there was only one way I wanted to do it with Teagan. The last few months had been the best of my entire life. We'd laughed and loved like I hadn't known was possible.

There was no doubt I wanted to spend the rest of my life with her, and it was time to make it official.

She gave me a kiss before taking her seat and reaching into her bowl of nuts. I had to sit back and exercise great patience. She gripped my hand on takeoff and only went back to snacking once we were airborne. I took the opportunity to close our private door.

She clicked through the entertainment options. "Ooh, they have the new Jennifer Anniston movie."

I loved her enthusiasm for the little things in life. It had made me appreciate everything I'd ever taken for granted.

"How are the nuts?" I asked and watched her grin light up her face.

"They're warm, salty, and— Hey, what's this?" She leaned over to take a look at what her fingers had found, lifting up a three-carat, emerald-cut diamond solitaire set in rose gold. Her big eyes searched mine.

"I thought of a dozen ways to ask you to marry me. The down-on-one-knee romantic setting with flowers didn't seem like us, but warm nuts on a plane did." God, I hoped I wasn't wrong. Maybe she'd have preferred the traditional form of proposal. I moved to get down on my knees.

"Don't you dare move," she whispered, still holding the ring with wide eyes.

"I took a chance with the rose gold because you're wrong

about pink not looking good on you. For instance, the blush staining your cheeks right now is the sexiest color I've ever seen on you. And don't get me started on my favorite pink lingerie set. But if you want—"

"I love the rose gold. It's the most exquisite ring I've ever seen."

"Does that mean you're saying yes to my nutty proposal?"

"Well, I don't remember you actually asking."

My brain did a quick rewind. "I didn't ask?"

She giggled. "I would've remembered a question like that."

Jesus, how fucking terrible could one be at a proposal? And here I'd thought about it for weeks and weeks. "I can't believe I messed this up."

"You see the huge grin on my face? You didn't mess anything up."

"I want a do-over."

"You got it." She took her hands, two fingers still clutching the ring, and chopped them together like a director's clapboard. "Proposal take two."

I took the ring from her fingers, holding it in mine. "I love you, Teagan, to the point of distraction given the way I forgot to actually ask you to marry me. These last eight months have been the best of my life. And I would be the luckiest man alive if you'd say yes to becoming my wife."

She smiled brilliantly. "Yes."

"Yes?"

"As if I'd say no to a man who would think to combine my two favorite things. Loving him and warm nuts."

I slid the ring on her left finger before leaning in to kiss right below her ear. "I thought neck kisses were your favorite thing."

"Mm, how could I forget?"

She climbed over the console to straddle my lap. "How soundproof do you think our cabin is?"

I pulled back to take in the mischievous glint in her eyes. "I have no clue, but there's no doubt we're about to find out."

Read the next book in the Miss Series! Tory and Chance's story is up next in Miss Trust.

ACKNOWLEDGMENTS

I hope you enjoyed reading about Teagan and Reid as much as I enjoyed writing them.

I want to take a moment to give a shout out to some of the people who make my books possible.

Alyssa Kress! You've been there since the very beginning and I couldn't do this without your valuable insight, important questions, and quick saves when it comes to my timing or things I may have goofed on!

Thank you to Kelly Green! For always being there whether it is it book related or not! You're such an important part of this journey!

To my amazing ARC team!!! You are so supportive and awesome!! Thank you for embracing this new series!

Thank you to my author friends! Elizabeth Kelly for her valuable beta reading skills. And Nikki Sloane for our sprint sessions!! This year has been challenging not to be distracted and it's so great to have fellow authors to talk about life, romance, and getting through the week!

Thank you to Marisa with Cover Me Darling for your gorgeous covers for this series.

To Judy of Judy's Proofreading, thank you for your eagle eyes!!

To Give Me Books: You guys are the best! Thank you for promoting my books, and having such a great team to work with!

To all of the amazing bloggers who shared Miss Belief, I thank you so much for your efforts!

And of course to my readers!! I adore you. You are the reason I can't wait to write the next book! Thank you for your enthusiasm and support!!!

ABOUT THE AUTHOR

Aubrey Bondurant is a working mom who loves to write, read, and travel.
She describes her writing style as: "Adult Contemporary Erotic Romantic Comedy," which is just another way of saying she likes her characters funny, her bedroom scenes hot, and her romances with a happy ending.
When Aubrey isn't working her day job or spending time with her family, she's on her laptop typing away on her next story. She only wishes there were more hours of the day!
She's a former member of the US Marine Corps and passionate about veteran charities and giving back to the community. She loves a big drooly dog, a fantastic margarita, and football.

Sign up for Aubrey's newsletter to get all of the latest information on new releases here

Join her FB Group
Follow her on Instagram
Email her at aubreybondurant@gmail.com

Printed in Great Britain
by Amazon